The Sheikh's Temporary Girlfriend
Mel Teshco

The Sheikh's Temporary Girlfriend
Copyright © 2023 Mel Teshco

Cover Art by HelzKat Designs
https://www.helzkatdesigns.com/

Chapter One

Amber Clayton hurried back to the bar and picked up yet another drinks tray holding ten crystal flutes of champagne. She swallowed hard as she walked carefully through the crowd of rich and famous, the men in formal suits and the women in dazzling evening gowns and priceless jewels.

She wasn't practiced in the art of drink carrying and had no idea how heavy ten glasses of champagne could get in a very short time, or how precarious they became as partygoers pushed past her.

Why was she doing this again?

Oh, yeah. She desperately needed the money to help bail out her brother, Zach from his latest gambling disaster. His wife had threatened to leave him and take their five year old child Katie with her if he didn't find a way to pay his accumulated debts...and soon.

Not that Amber blamed her sister-in-law, Rachel. She must have been shattered when she'd discovered how deeply Zach had gotten himself into debt. Rachel had been completely unaware of her husband's gambling problem, her trust now as broken as Zach's addiction.

Amber's daytime gig at the local surf school might be her dream job, but it was far and away from the best paying and wouldn't even put a dent in what her brother owed. Not even his skill as an accountant would save him from financial disaster.

A soap opera star in pearls and a tight gold sequined dress plucked a flute from off the tray, making two other flutes wobble. "Finally!" she complained in an aggrieved voice, her brunette hair long and perfectly straight and her blue eyes glacial.

Resisting the need to pat down her barely restrained blonde riot of curls, Amber sent the woman a strained smile and continued to weave around the glittering throng of Sheikh Basam's guests, all the while heading in his direction. He was, after all, the man paying for the get-together.

Though he was renowned for paying his wait-staff well, the icing on the cake was the nice fat bonus he dished out if the party was a success. She only hoped and prayed that it *was*.

Anything to help keep Zach and his family together.

Her stomach clenched. She and Zach had already lost their parents in a car accident five years ago. If Katie disappeared from their life too, it would kill them both.

It's Zach's stupid fault. Maybe losing Katie will teach him a lesson once and for all.

She scrubbed the thought from her mind. He was her brother, and despite his ghastly gambling addiction, she loved him. She wouldn't stand by and see him lose everything, including the woman he loved along with his precious daughter.

Amber's supervisor waddled through the crowd toward her, his face flushed and his shirt too-tight for his bull neck. "What are you doing? Get those drinks to Sheikh Basam *now!*"

She smiled tightly. If she didn't need this job so badly she'd tell the rude, bullfrog of a man to go to hell. But she *did* need this job and she'd put up with a lot worse to get her pay and a bonus. "I'm heading over there now."

"Hurry up, then. And see to it that you give him your prettiest smile."

She bit back a retort as she continued to weave through the crowd. She wasn't here to look pretty. She was here to do a job and do it well. A shame the heeled shoes she'd borrowed from Rachel were half-a-size too small and were already killing her feet. Between that and her aching shoulders and arms she was ready to kick off her shoes, throw down her tray and subside against the nearest wall while giving into tears of self-pity.

"Careful!"

The word of warning came too late. A clearly drunk, careless young man lurched heavily against her before he disappeared into the crowd. Her drinks tray tilted one way, the champagne glasses teetering. She managed to rebalance the tray, but it was too late for the flutes of champagne. They toppled sideways, splashing the dark gray business suit and immaculate white shirt of the man in front of her before crashing to the floor in an explosion of crystal glass.

Amber froze as the crowd audibly gasped. She slowly lifted her eyes. *Sheikh Basam.*

His eyes narrowed and her throat restricted, becoming so tight she couldn't have issued an apology if she tried. If his infamy wasn't clear enough, his height and silent strength most certainly were. Add his predatory dark golden eyes that made her feel like prey, along with his dark designer stubble that highlighted his aquiline nose and high cheekbones, and she couldn't help but take an involuntary step back.

Her supervisor appeared from out of the crowd. He sucked in a horrified breath before it spluttered back out again in a rush. "I'm so very sorry Sheikh Basam. Amber is new, a substitute for another staff member who came down sick."

Sheikh Basam ignored her supervisor. All Basam's attention seemed centered entirely on her. "Amber," he murmured with a speculative gaze. He glanced down at his soggy jacket and shirt. "I'd say it was a pleasure to meet you, but I'm not yet sure that's entirely true."

She gulped, his accented voice and fathomless regard pulling at her despite her anxiety. "I-I'm so sorry. I'm not usually so clumsy."

Her confession had her supervisor puff up like a rooster condemning one of his hens. "Let me reassure you, Sheikh Basam, the dry-cleaning will come out of her pay."

She wilted at his words, her lashes sweeping low as tears sprung to her eyes. Such an expense would cost her hundreds, perhaps even thousands. Her night here was heading toward a complete disaster and might well see her having a bill instead of a much needed wage.

"That's not necessary," Sheikh Basam refuted coolly. "I can afford my own dry cleaning."

"Thank you," she said in a tremulous voice. "You don't know how much that means to me."

His gaze darkened. "I'm beginning to think that I do." He smiled gently. "If anything, the bill should be coming out of the intoxicated young man who almost knocked you off your feet."

"You saw that?" she asked weakly.

He nodded. "I tried to warn you. Unfortunately, it was too little, too late."

Her supervisor rounded on her. "I hope you're grateful that you came out of this unscathed."

"I am—"

"Either way, I'm afraid your services are no longer needed here tonight," the toad-of-a-man interjected.

Her chest expanded as outrage filled her. "You can't be serious?"

"I don't make empty threats." Her supervisor sniffed heavily. "Of course, accidents do happen," he allowed.

You were just unlucky that it was a sheikh you spilled a tray of drinks on.

He didn't need to state the obvious. The sheikh had come over to Australia for a mini-break to meet some esteemed guests. The Queensland island he'd chosen to stay for his last night wasn't meant to be memorable for all the wrong reasons.

The sheikh crossed his arms. "Before you chase this young lady off for good, I'd like to have a chat with her first."

Her supervisor blinked in surprise, then acquiesced with a nod. "Of course, Sheikh Basam."

Amber gaped. "A ch-chat?"

Why would the sheikh need to speak to her? Surely a few spilled drinks didn't warrant a lecture? *Shit.* Was he going to dock her pay, after all?

The sheikh smiled and held out the crook of his arm for her to clasp. She obeyed without even thinking, and glass crunched under her heeled shoes as she left the room, which was now buzzing openly with speculation.

A team of cleaners swooped in to get rid of the mess even as he guided her outside through automated glass sliding doors. Her heels *click-clacked* as they descended a dozen, wide concrete steps, which led into a garden rich with the sweet scent of frangipani and overlaid with briny salt air.

She'd yet to take the time to notice how spectacular the garden was at nighttime, where solar lights highlighted big leafy palms and flowering trees.

He slowed before he turned to face her, and she blinked up at him, his shadowed face somehow making him even more imposing. She managed a smile. "Wouldn't this be considered a little inappropriate in your country?"

"Perhaps," he conceded, his accented voice as smooth and silken as honey. "Except we're not in my country. We're in your western world where women have far more freedom." He cocked his head to the side. "Though whether that gives you more happiness or not is questionable."

She dropped her hand from his arm. "We all have our problems, Sheikh Basam. I'm sure even with all your money you have troubles of your own."

"Please, call me Basam. And yes, you're right. I do have my own...complications, just as it seems you have yours."

The garden no longer felt enchanted. All her problems seemed a hundredfold now, brought to the forefront of her mind by his candid honesty. "I'd be lying if I said I didn't."

"Then perhaps we can help each other."

Amber felt dizzy suddenly and more than a little faint. "How on Earth do you think I can help *you*?"

"I need someone suitable to be my girlfriend—my *pretend* girlfriend."

A giggle escaped her as hysteria threatened. "You're kidding me, right?" At his somber, all too serious face, she added, "I mean, you'd have women falling over themselves just to be seen with you let alone being your girlfriend—pretend or otherwise!"

"And therein lays the problem. I don't want a woman who imagines herself in some fairytale love story. What I need is a woman desperate enough to play the game and keep up the pretense, then walk away at the finish of the week with her end of the bargain intact."

That she'd also need to keep her heart intact seemed to have slipped his mind, no doubt because she'd had desperation written all over her face. Her broken finances made her the perfect candidate as his malleable girlfriend.

"One week?"

He nodded. "Seven days is all that I ask."

"But—why?"

"A very good friend of my late father has every expectation that I'll now marry his daughter."

"And you're not yet ready to settle down?"

He pushed a hand over his face. "Let's just say she's not my type."

"Is she *that* unattractive?" She couldn't stop a note of bitterness from creeping into her voice. She had enough experience with men to know they were attracted to her blonde good looks and her bikini-toned body. A pity none had stuck around long enough to fall for her inner beauty.

"I wouldn't say that," he hedged.

She curled her lip. "But you're not denying it, either."

He sighed heavily. "All I want to hear from you right now is a *yes* or *no*." Her entire body tensed, and about to tell him to go to hell, he added succinctly, "Name your price."

"Name my price?" she echoed weakly. Was he serious? But of course he was—he was a sheikh, no doubt he had unlimited funds. "Just what exactly is involved in this...charade?"

"I want you to pretend to be in love with me, totally smitten. We both need to be. Anything less and our...relationship just won't work."

"But what about your guests? I don't doubt the rumors are already spreading like wildfire about us. An island won't stop the lies."

He arched a knowing brow. "They'll be saying I couldn't take my eyes off you from the moment you deliberately spilled drinks on me. They'll also say there was instant chemistry between us."

"Love at first sight?" she asked drily, even as her heart banged against her ribs in sudden wishful thinking.

"It happens, apparently."

Her mind whirled. What was the catch? It all seemed too easy. "Will we be sharing a bed?"

"For the sake of my gossiping servants, yes, we'll have to share a bed." At her shocked inhalation, he added, "But I don't expect sex. Not unless you want it, of course."

"No sex," she amended firmly, her nipples springing into tight buds at the vision that suddenly sprang to mind: his strong legs tangled around hers, their mouths fused along with their hot and sweaty, naked bodies. She cleared her throat and held his stare. "And one-hundred-thousand dollars upfront."

"Deal."

"Deal?" she echoed yet again. He'd agreed *that* easily to her price.

He nodded. "Just one thing."

"Yes?"

He leaned close, and as if in slow motion, he moved his hands behind her head before his soft lips closed over her mouth. Electricity danced between them as her dormant nerve endings fired into life. She moaned into his mouth, weak-kneed at his skill.

How was she going to be able to resist him if they shared a bed for seven nights straight? His kiss was drugging, addicting, his hands around her nape a dominant touch that made her want to lean into him and allow him to strip away her defenses, take away every single one of her troubles in the world.

He pulled back, his dark golden eyes glinting and his voice husky. "I thought we should seal the deal with a kiss." He smiled, his teeth bright white under the solar lights. "I'll pick you up from your room in the morning at eight o'clock sharp. Be ready."

"Eight o'clock!" She blinked up at him, the sharp, fruity scent of champagne splattered on his clothes surely intoxicating her and scrambling her brain? "I need more time!"

"Your payment will be in your bank account within the hour. You don't need any more time. Tomorrow is the start of your first day on the job...and your seven day contract. Be ready, Amber."

He walked away with a fluid, pantherish gait she found mesmerizing. Or maybe she was too stunned to move knowing all her worries had been solved in one foul swoop.

Have they, though? Or have you just made things a whole lot more complicated?

She forced her legs to move. No regrets. She'd do whatever had to be done to save her brother's marriage and to keep his daughter. After all, Zach had done whatever he'd had to for her after their parents had died. Not only had he comforted her, he'd supported her both emotionally and financially.

It was time to return the favor.

Chapter Two

Amber paced back and forth in her tiny motel room that was reserved exclusively for paid staff, and although the sun had cracked the horizon outside, giving the sky a soft, rosy-tinged glow, it did little to soothe her state of mind.

She'd been conjuring up hundreds of worst case scenarios. What if the sheikh kidnapped her and never allowed her to return home? What if this was some kind of elaborate scheme designed to get her out of her own country and into his before she was sex trafficked or worse?

What if you and your brother never see Katie again?

Her fear subsided, strength coursing through her veins. Nothing was too big a risk when it came to the possibility of losing her niece.

She'd had a hard time on the phone last night trying to explain to her brother that his debts would be settled. He'd been disbelieving, then overjoyed, then deeply suspicious. At her cajoling he'd become cautiously optimistic, even while he'd asked over and over again where she'd possibly found the money.

In the end she'd told him she'd hit the jackpot. It hadn't been a lie, not really. She *had* hit the jackpot, just not in the way he'd imagined. That he'd believed her gambling had solved his debts left a sour taste in her mouth, but there was little to be done about it now.

He would have used every trick in his arsenal to not let her leave Australia and go to some foreign country with a virtual stranger. She might no longer be a child, but he was still a protective older brother.

She went into the bathroom and wet her hands before pressing them to her warm brow. Her dark blue eyes—the color of the ocean, according to her niece—flashed with another bout of misgiving. What if—

Knock. Knock.

Her throat dried, her heart pitter-pattering as she forced her legs to carry her out of the bathroom and to the front door. She touched her tightly bound hair—it would be a wild mass of blonde curls if she left it unrestrained—before she smoothed a hand over her long yellow sundress with its embossed triangular print. Though it was fitted at the bodice and waist, it flared out to flow loosely to her ankles.

It was her most modest dress. She didn't own any Middle-Eastern type clothes. She was a beach girl, less was more. Comfort was top priority. Her entire wardrobe was probably considered indecent by the sheikh and his people's standards.

She unlatched the tiny, inadequate chain-lock that was meant to keep her safe, then pulled open the motel door. Her pulse surged. Sheikh Basam was delectable. His white dress shirt enhanced his sun-kissed skin, his broad shoulders and spare torso, while his fawn pants hugged his lean waist and powerful thighs. His outfit probably cost more than her sedan she'd left parked inside her garage.

Behind him a shiny dark SUV waited, while a middle-aged man in a formal suit and black cap with visor stood beside its open passenger door.

"Amber," the sheikh murmured. "I'm happy to see you this morning." At her unblinking gaze he explained, "I thought you might have changed your mind."

And lose Katie? Never!

She lifted her chin. "I don't make a habit of going back on my word."

He smiled as he handed her some paperwork. "Then you will want to read and sign this contract before we leave."

"Contract?" she repeated weakly.

"Yes. I had my lawyer put it together late last night."

"Of course you did," she said, stepping aside to let him in before she shut the door and followed with the paperwork. "Would you like coffee or tea?"

"No, thank you." He nodded at the paperwork. "If you could read and sign the paperwork, then we can leave."

He was clearly in a hurry. She guessed seven days was a bit of a stretch to try and convince someone he was in love with another woman. That Amber was a commoner Australian would surely be pushing the believability factor to the limit?

She inwardly shrugged. It wasn't her concern. She'd do her best to play her part. The rest was up to Basam and his acting ability.

She sat at the little round table, reading everything twice over. Though there were plenty of technical words, there was nothing out of order. Nothing more than what Sheikh Basam had asked of her.

He sat at the other side of the table, his presence big and commanding, and seemingly sucking away all the oxygen. Her hands shook slightly as she signed the contract and slid it his way. "Done."

He nodded, then pulled a velvet box from the pocket of his pants. "We're not quite done here yet." He opened the lid with his long, blunt-ended fingers and she gasped at the exquisite diamond choker and matching drop earrings inside. His eyes glinted. "I want you to put these on before we leave."

"They're beautiful."

He smiled. "They're yours."

"Mine?" she croaked.

He nodded. "Yes. You get to keep them after our seven days end."

The room did a slow spin. They had to cost a small fortune, probably more than the sum she'd requested that would delete her brother's bills once and for all. "You're serious, aren't you?"

"I am." He stood and stepped behind her. "I don't make jokes when it comes to my future," he said softly, decisively.

With her frizzy hair already in a bun, he had no difficulty putting the choker around her throat. A hot shiver spiraled through her at the touch of his hand on her flesh, and her hands shook a little as she put in the earrings.

He stepped back. "Perfect," he mused huskily.

If only the next seven days would be this simple. But she had a sneaking suspicion her time with the sheikh would be a whole lot more complicated.

His stare gleamed. "Everyone will know these are a gift from me."

She nodded. Of course they would. She certainly couldn't afford jewels of any kind, and these were worth a fortune. The sheikh wanted everyone to believe their relationship was serious from the get-go.

She withheld a sigh. She was living every girl's fantasy, never mind that it was under false pretenses.

With the paperwork signed and the expensive gift around her neck and in her lobes, Basam glanced at her one small suitcase near her bedroom door. "That is all you're taking?"

"I travel light," she hedged. He didn't need to know her clothes were mostly shorts and singlets, with jeweled flip-flops her favorite accessory.

"I'll arrange to get anything else you might need," he said as he crossed the room in a couple of strides and grabbed her undersized suitcase with big hands.

She stepped outside, a seagull squawking as it floated overhead on the briny sea breeze. She climbed into the back seat with the sheikh, thankful that no one appeared to be out and about at this early hour of the morning. Most of the guests would be hungover and sleeping in after the unlimited booze from the night before.

But she didn't doubt the rumors would be in full force by the end of the day.

Not even ten minutes later she climbed out of the SUV and into a waiting helicopter that flew them to the mainland airport, and within walking distance to the sheikh's private jet. After traversing the tarmac and climbing the steps, she gawped openly at the stunning leather seats and spaciousness of the lounge and bar area.

"There is a bedroom in the back if you're tired," he informed her.

Her chest tightened and her mind ran rampant. *Damn it!* Why did she think such sexual thoughts around the sheikh? Yes, he was as sexy as hell, but she'd known a lot of too-handsome men in her day.

That not one of them had his kind of charisma was beside the point, wasn't it?

A pretty brunette air hostess walked toward them. "Sheikh Basam, would you or your guest like a drink or something to eat while the pilot prepares for takeoff?"

"A fruit snack and something non-alcoholic," he glanced at Amber and added, "for my girlfriend Amber, and myself."

If the air hostess was shocked she didn't let on, she was coolly professional and kept any thoughts about his latest girlfriend to herself. Basam obviously paid her well.

Amber's heart did a dull thud in her chest. Perhaps the sheikh should have asked the brunette to be his girlfriend for the next seven days?

She shook off the thought. Basam had chosen her and she refused to question his logic any further. It was enough that all her brother's financial woes would soon be behind him—behind them both since his financial concerns had become hers. She'd do her best to simply enjoy the ride while she was on it.

The snack turned out to be the sweetest strawberries Amber might ever had eaten, along with swirls of fresh cream and shaved dark chocolate served in a tall glass with a spoon. Once finished, she sipped on a glass of fizzy grape juice, an amazing concoction that undoubtedly cost a truckload.

Basam moved closer, then clasped her hand and lifted it to his mouth. She stared as he kissed her knuckles, electricity dancing through her nerve endings while butterflies fluttered in her stomach.

She blinked and he smiled and murmured, "I thought we'd better start practicing our great love for one another or no one will believe our attraction is real."

Great love? People like him didn't find great love with people like her. She cleared her throat, almost too weak to snatch her hand from his hold. "I have faith in my acting abilities."

His smile turned into a wide grin. "I'm counting on it, sunshine."

"Sunshine?"

He nodded. "A man should have a pet name for his sweetheart, don't you think?"

Her senses went into overdrive and she almost swayed toward him. This was make-believe, none of this was real! She jerked back, her lips pressed together. "Is that the best you could come up with?"

He lifted a hand and touched her hair. "Would you prefer spun-sugar? Because that is also what your hair reminds me of."

"Sunshine is fine!" she said in a high-pitched squeak, suddenly breathless by his compliments. He was a sheikh! Wasn't she supposed to be giving him the accolades?

"I didn't mean to make you nervous," he said, his tawny eyes sweeping over her heated face. "You have nothing to fear. Nothing happens between us unless you want it."

"Good."

He nodded, his smile a little crooked.

Did he imagine she'd give into his prowess sooner rather than later? She frowned. It made her want to dig her heels in even harder to ensure she wasn't just another of his women in a long line of many.

Despite her inner conflict and need, weariness was catching up on her fast. She stifled a yawn. These seven days couldn't be behind her fast enough.

At some point she must have dozed off because she woke to the world tilting around her as Basam laid her onto a bed in the jet's bedroom. A strange little thrill went through her at seeing him looking down at her with his golden eyes, as though he wanted to kiss her again...as though he wanted to do far more than that but respected her boundaries.

"Sleep, sunshine. You have a big seven days in front of you."

It felt weirdly right when he pressed his lips to her brow. When he retreated it took everything she had not to call him back. She frowned, then sighed heavily, her lashes already drooping with the jet engines constant drone. He was right. She *was* exhausted.

She woke to what she presumed must be hours later after having the most restful, dreamless sleep she'd had in a long time. She'd been so stressed about her brother and his family it'd been affecting her sleep quality in a big way.

She sat and looked around, unsure whether to be relieved or disappointed that Basam was nowhere to be seen. At least it gave her a chance to take in the sumptuousness of the bedroom. Though the walls were accented in black, the soft lighting made the space seem much bigger, as did the sculptural lights above her that were presently dimmed low. The white bed sheets and cover with a black throw was a lovely, if not masculine touch, one that seemed perfect for Basam.

The only feminine touches were the white orchids with red rosebuds and green fernery in a vase that sat in a deep inset on a side table. Then she noticed the big fruit and cheese platter on the end of the bed, her stomach immediately rumbling.

The door opened and Basam entered with a bottle of champagne and two glasses. He smiled. "Good, you're awake. We'll be landing in a few hours, but I thought you might want to eat and freshen up first."

She blinked. "Don't we need to fuel up somewhere first?"

He laughed. "Already done. You slept like a log through the whole process."

"H-how long was I asleep?"

"All day and most of the night."

"Seriously?" It meant she only had six days now to get through. Six days to convince his closest friends and staff—not to mention his people—that she was in love with him.

He sat, placing the champagne glasses next to the vase of flowers on the side table before he cracked open the chilled glass bottle. "You clearly needed the sleep."

"I did," she admitted.

He nodded. "I had the chef mix a little herbal sleeping concoction to go into your drink."

She gasped. "You *what?*"

"Don't sound so shocked. You desperately needed to sleep, and I gave it to you. I didn't drug you with a dangerous prescription medication, you were perfectly safe."

"You might have raped me!" she burst out.

He stiffened. "Believe me—if or when—we get together, it will be a mutual decision or not at all. It will never be one-sided."

She bit her lip, her face flushing. If he thought for one second she'd give into his advances, he could think again! It mattered little that her mind conjured up graphic images of them naked and twisting the sheets in the throes of passion. "That doesn't excuse you for drugging me."

"It was a natural sleeping draught." He cocked is head to the side. "I don't know what it is you might have heard about me, but non-consensual sex is one act I will never condone."

She nodded slowly, tension unwinding inside her. "I believe you."

"Good," he popped the cork, "because without your trust our arrangement won't work." He poured them each a glass of champagne, then handed one to her. His stare held hers as he lifted his glass in a toast. "To our fake partnership."

She lifted her glass to clink it against his, her hand surprisingly shaky as the full extent of her commitment suddenly hit her.

What had she done?

Chapter Three

Amber and Basam devoured the fruit and cheese platter while they sipped on champagne and talked of inconsequential things that nevertheless showcased Basam's intelligence. He was highly educated, his life experiences making him even more cultivated.

She probably looked like something between a country hick and a beach bum in comparison.

She swallowed the last of her champagne. Though she'd had too much to drink, she needed whatever courage she could find knowing what was ahead of her. His people would be judging her, and no doubt the dignitaries would be even worse as they looked down their long noses at her.

"Would you like to take a shower and freshen up before we land?" he asked.

She shook her head. "I'll wait until we get to the palace."

He didn't need to know she had nothing else suitable to wear.

He left then to make use of the shower himself in the adjoining bathroom. It had to be the alcohol that made her so tempted to follow him. Even worse were the erotic visuals that played through her head at the thought of the rivulets of hot water running over his sculptured, naked body. His clothes didn't hide the hard planes of his body, no matter how much she tried not to notice.

Her hands trembled a little when she applied some fresh pink gloss to her lips and redid her hair before tying it up securely. If this was how strongly her emotions were at the start of this pretense with Basam, what would they be like by day seven?

Sucking in a steadying breath, she left the bedroom and returned to the window seat, clipping on her belt as the jet quickly descended toward the private runway. She looked out the tinted windows to the barren desert landscape below. Though the sun was just cracking the horizon, it was still dark enough outside to see the myriad of lights in the distance. No doubt it was the city where Basam resided.

He returned dressed in a white thobe and keffiyeh headwear. She stared at him. If he was gorgeous in western clothes, his traditional outfit sent shivers down her spine. He looked taller and even more formidable, a true king of the desert.

"Keep staring at me like that and I won't be held accountable for my actions."

She lifted her chin. "And what actions would that be?"

His eyes all but glowed, not unlike a tiger stalking its prey. "I think you know exactly what I mean, sunshine."

"And I think you must remember what I said."

He nodded. "Yes. *No sex.* Those words are printed indelibly into my brain."

"Good." She turned away before he saw the uncertainty in her eyes. Because suddenly she wasn't so sure about her self-imposed rule, she was convinced more than ever that she wanted to be with a man like Basam. She was just as convinced that the boys she'd dated in the past wouldn't compare.

They finally touched-down, the pilot landing the jet as smooth as butter. It wasn't until he'd taxied it down the runway and toward a building she assumed was a hangar that she noticed the small crowd waiting for their arrival. As the jet got closer she realized by the cameras and microphones those same people were reporters.

She turned to Basam. "Were you aware of the press waiting for us?"

He frowned, then leaned closer to her to take a look out the window. He swore emphatically. "Someone must have leaked the news."

She gulped, trying not to notice his bulk so close to hers. But it was impossible to ignore his magnetism and power. He radiated both. "Who could possibly know?"

"You'd be surprised." He nodded at her choker and earrings. "It wouldn't be the first time someone hid in the bushes and zoomed their camera on me or anyone close to me—anything they could use as news. In our case it would be my gift to you. The gutter-press are piranhas who'd gladly draw blood to make a story."

She touched her choker. "Then I guess the jewelry did its job."

He sighed heavily. "Yes, though I was hoping you'd be shielded for a few more days yet from a mob of news-hungry reporters."

A pair of guards in matching thobes with firearms at their sides materialized from where they'd been sitting at the front of the jet plane. Fear for a moment held her spellbound before logic reasserted itself. They were here to protect their sheikh, which meant by association, they'd protect her too. That she hadn't seen them for the entire trip meant they had to be good at their jobs to stay so invisible and unobtrusive.

"Are you ready for this?" Basam asked.

No! She nodded. "Yes."

That she was so desperately unprepared left her stomach twisting with nausea. He wanted her to put on the best act of her life, but she'd have to do an Oscar winning performance to get out of these seven days unscathed, not to mention get people to believe they were in deeply in love.

The same brunette air hostess opened the door to the steps outside, her smile as bright as her obvious devotion to Basam. "I hope you enjoyed your flight today, Sheikh Basam." Her smile dropped a little as she added, "Amber."

Amber hid a frown and decided now was as good a time as any to test out her acting skills. Looking up at Basam with what she hoped was pure adoration; she said huskily, "I did always wonder about the Mile High Club." She giggled. "At least now I no longer have to use my imagination."

She stood on tiptoes and pressed her lips to Basam's. For an infinitesimal second he stiffened, as though shocked by her outright lie and the sudden desire to show off their fake passion for one another. Then he groaned and returned her kiss, dominated it, his skill unparalleled to anything she'd experienced before.

This wasn't just a kiss filled with excitement and danger; it was an exchange of trust, of belief in one another. The electric current that zapped through her body and made her toes curl was nothing more than a lovely fringe benefit.

The air hostess gaped, but Amber was becoming too lost in sensation to care. Basam's lips might be pillowy and soft, but his mouth was hard and uncompromising. He wasn't shy in getting what he wanted.

She might have taken the first step, but he'd be the one to finish it.

A flash of bright lights tore them apart, leaving her blinking at the people behind the cameras on the tarmac below. That they'd captured the intimate moment between her and the sheikh for a moment made her sick with shock. Except this was what he'd wanted, wasn't it? A pity her act hadn't been an act, not as far as her body was concerned.

It'd been fully invested in their kiss.

Basam leaned down, his warm breath stirring her nerve endings once again as he whispered in her ear, "I'm impressed."

It took everything she had not to demand a repeat kiss and impress him even more. Instead she smiled up at him and said sweetly, "One day down, six to go."

She wasn't quite sure how to interpret his unyielding face and suddenly unreadable gaze at her words. All she knew for sure was that she much preferred the admiring gaze he'd lavished on her just seconds before she'd opened her mouth and reminded him of their contract.

Then he nodded and murmured, "Indeed," before he ushered her forward, out of his private jet and down the stairs leading to the tarmac and the voices shouting out questions even before they'd fully alighted.

"Sheikh Basam. Is this your girlfriend?"

"What do you have to say about the rumors of your love affair with a waitress?"

"Can you confirm or deny your story?"

"Sources corroborate you've been seeing one another for months. Is that true?"

Amber resisted cringing and instead lifting her hand to touch her choker. "Hi everyone, I'm Amber. It's a pleasure to meet you all."

Shock for a moment held her audience still, then they all spoke at once, a gaggle of voices that surrounded her and Basam as they moved toward their waiting car. The guards intervened then, ensuring their sheikh and Amber had safe passage through the mob and into the backseat of their chauffeured black stretch sedan.

As the car slid forward and left the reporters behind, Amber closed her eyes and leaned her head back against the buttery leather seat. She blew out an unsteady breath. "Wow. That was intense."

"Yet you handled it like a pro."

She flicked open her eyes and tilted her head to stare up at him. Damn he was gorgeous. It seemed unfair that someone in a robe and headgear could appear even more masculine and powerful. "So why do you sound so unhappy? Did I do something wrong?"

"On the contrary, you did everything right."

She relaxed just a little, though she knew he wasn't being entirely truthful. Then again, their whole being together was an act so she shouldn't be surprised. "At least I get to prepare myself for a few hours before I face the people of your palace."

"A few hours?" He chuckled darkly, amused by her words. "Hardly."

"What do you mean? You *do* live in the city I saw in the distance from the air, don't you?"

He shook his head. "What you saw was the nearest city to my desert palace."

"Desert palace?" she said weakly.

He nodded and swept out a languid hand to indicate the sealed road ahead, the manmade development making the desert either side look even more desolate and wild. "While the city is three hours' drive away, it's little more than a ten minute drive from my private airport to my palace."

Her stomach tightened. "So I'll be practically living in the desert for six days?"

"Yes." He smiled indulgently. "But don't stress, sunshine. I have all the amenities you could ever want there."

"Does that include a beach?"

"We *do* have all the sand you could ever want."

His amusement didn't stop a sudden longing to breathe in crisp salty air while standing on the pristine sandy shore of the Pacific Ocean, watching the ceaseless waves roll in and crash into white foam, while the seagulls wheeled in the breeze above the glistening deep-blue water.

Her hands clenched to her sides. It'd been one day and she was already craving the wet sand between her toes and the hot sun on her bikini-clad body. How was she going to feel shrouded in the abayas she had no doubt would be provided for her?

Then Basam put his hand on her thigh, the electric surge that charged through her somehow dissolving all her doubts. "I'm certain these seven days won't leave you disappointed."

Not if he had anything to do with it. He didn't have to say the words. She could all but hear them hanging in the air between them.

"I'm counting on it," she said softly.

Their vehicle cleared a bit of a rise, enabling her to see ahead to a huge, white palace. Her breath caught in her throat. She hadn't expected it to be so...magnificent! It was like a small city in itself, with a wall enclosing the many domes and spheres along with its outbuildings.

If he noticed her shock he didn't comment. Instead he said huskily, "I'm counting on it too, sunshine."

Chapter Four

Amber couldn't help but feel overwhelmed as she walked hand-in-hand with Basam past his guards, one pair who were stationed at the entrance of his palace and another pair at the front of his private wing, where he appeared to enjoy relative seclusion inside his suite of rooms.

If the whole palace was beautiful with its mosaic floors in bold diamond patterns and glittering chandeliers that hung from domed ceilings, then Basam's suite of rooms were sumptuous.

He opened double doors to a sitting room, no doubt where visitors were kept from the rest of his suite when needed. She followed him through an arched doorway into a hallway, where another door opened into a lounge room with big comfortable chairs facing a big screen television. A gleaming, mahogany bar took up a corner of the room, and at the opposite end a dining room showcased a round marble table with damask-covered chairs.

She did a slow turn. "My whole apartment would fit into this room."

He sent her an assessing look and acknowledged, "There are benefits to being rich."

She arched a brow and said wryly, "I wouldn't know."

He nodded toward a set of double doors set back into another hallway. "Our bedroom is through there."

Our bedroom.

She swallowed past a suddenly dry throat, her imagination once again taking her to places she didn't want to go. *Shouldn't* want to go. He'd only asked her to play this role because she was desperate for money. She would *not* be desperate for him. She wouldn't self-sabotage and be just another weak-willed, panting woman ready to throw away all self-respect just to be with him.

Her feet sank into the thick cream carpet of their bedroom, where a canopied, four-poster bed took center stage. Embroidered, champagne-colored curtains framed large tinted windows that looked out to a garden courtyard, a sitting area with more damask covered chairs taking advantage of the views outside.

As servants brought in their luggage and unpacked it all into a huge walk-in closet, Basam showed her the rest of the suite, which included an intimate cinema to watch the latest blockbusters.

Her eyes bulged as they walked into the next room, this one long and rectangular. "You have your own indoor lap pool in the middle of the desert?"

He smiled at her awed disbelief. "Believe me, it's one indulgence I couldn't live without. I swim laps most days when I'm home."

"Stress relief?" she asked.

He nodded. "It also keeps me fit and my mind sharp."

"Most guys have a home gym for that."

"I have one of those too. Feel free to use it or the pool whenever we're not busy with social engagements."

His reminder of why exactly she was here took away a little of the shine. But then she had to remember how many other girls would pinch themselves just to be here in such luxurious surroundings, a palace no less, while pretending to be a hot sheikh's girlfriend.

She might live each day like it was a holiday by residing in the tropics and working at the beach, surfing and swimming in sparkling blue ocean water...but when had she actually taken a trip to some other exotic location? The last holiday she'd taken had been to Sydney to visit a friend. Her lips curled. And she and her friend had spent most of their time at Bondi Beach.

Basam drew her out into the paved, garden courtyard, where big date palms shaded some garden seats and plants that spilled out of big pots. Water burbled from a fountain between two copper statues of children with baskets that held some kind of fernery, a deliciously cool breeze taking away much of the vicious morning heat.

"It's more comfortable out here in the late afternoon," he said conversationally.

She smiled. "I'm used to the heat. The only thing missing is the sand and ocean."

"I can't help you with the ocean, but Mother Nature does occasionally deliver on the latter when we get a sandstorm. Then you'll find it everywhere—inside and out—of the palace."

"You must have a competent cleaning crew. I've yet to see a speck of dust or a grain of sand in any of your rooms."

"My servants take pride in keeping my palace impeccable."

"Or perhaps they're terrified you'll find fault and rain down your wrath?"

He arched a dark brow. "I'm not a monster, Amber. If I was I would have made you pay for spilling those glasses of champagne on me."

"Isn't that why I'm here now?" she asked.

His gaze darkened. "Does being here *feel* like punishment?" he asked silkily.

She sighed. "No, of course not. In all honesty, I feel blessed that I'm here." *And that I'm able to pay off my brother's debts.*

Basam's gaze sharpened, but he didn't push the matter. Instead he drew her back inside his suite of rooms. "I asked for lunch to be brought here." At her relieved sigh, he added, "I guessed you might like a few more hours to prepare yourself before your first official meeting at dinner tonight."

Her insides went jittery. "There will be important people at your dinner table tonight?"

"Yes." He frowned. "That *is* what our agreement entailed."

He was right. Of course he was right. She'd already spent a day on his plane—mostly sleeping—and so far day two hadn't been all that bad, either. Not unless she counted meeting the press, but even that hadn't too overwhelming. She'd managed to hold her own with them.

She nodded. "That's...fair. I'm sure I'll do fine tonight, maybe even win some kind of award for my acting." She cleared her throat. "Just as long as you fill me in on any customs I should know about and the people I'll be meeting tonight so I'll at least be informed...or forewarned."

"I'll tell you everything you need to know at lunch. Then afterward a dressmaker will be arriving to fit you with some new clothes."

She blinked, relieved to hear it, despite him seemingly taking control of her every waking moment. She huffed out a breath. He'd taken control of her sleeping moments too. That she felt better for it was beside the point! *Whatever*. She really did need some clothes that were suitable for her role. "You've thought of everything."

He smirked. "I didn't get this successful by not thinking ahead."

Just how successful was he? He must be loaded for the upkeep of his palace alone, let alone the wages he'd pay for all his servants and staff. She'd bet the palace wasn't his only property. He probably owned plenty of other assets and businesses.

A knock sounded on the front door and Basam opened it before a chef in full whites pushed a trolley through. "Sheikh Basam," the chef said with a respectful little bow. "I personally cooked you and your visitor a lunch banquet."

Basam nodded approval. "Perfect. Thank you, Samuel."

Her eyes popped wide apart, but she kept her mouth shut as the chef than set out some dishes along with two bottles of accompanying wines onto the dining table. "Enjoy," he said, before he took his leave.

The scent of spiced aromas filled the room and her stomach gurgled. But though she was hungry, she held Basam's gaze and asked, "Was that Samuel Conray—*the* reality television chef?"

Basam nodded. "I take it you've watched his cooking shows?"

"Are you kidding me? His Middle East cooking opened my eyes to the fact there is more than doner-kebabs to be enjoyed after a few too many drinks on a Saturday night."

"Doner-kebabs?" he laughed. "Most of us enjoy shawarma here. The dish is similar but much more spiced and flavorsome in my opinion." He pulled out a seat for her. "It seems you have much to learn about my country and its people."

She accepted the proffered seat. "Not to mention the food," she conceded. "I can't wait to taste the real deal."

Basam lifted the lid to what appeared to be a casserole. "Thareed. Lamb, butternut squash, onion, broth and spices." He ladled some of it into a bowl for her, then advised, "This is best mopped up with naan bread."

She tasted the fragrant dish. "Yum."

He smiled and uncovered the other dishes while giving a running commentary, "Kibbeh, which is essentially a fried beef cake. Fattoush. Mixed greens with crunchy, fried bread pieces. Tabouleh. You might have had something similar in your doner-kebabs."

"I did, though whether it was authentic like what your chef makes, I have no idea." She swallowed some more of the thareed, and moaned. "All I know is I want to try a little bit of everything."

"Then a little bit of everything you shall have," he declared.

Half-an-hour later, Amber's stomach was so full she could burst, while her brain was so overloaded with his country's customs it threatened to burst right along with it. Taking one last sip of wine, she sat back and belched politely behind her hand. "Pardon me."

Basam's laugh was warm enough to send tingles up her spine even before he sat back and murmured, "You really are precious, sunshine."

She grinned. "You're that easily impressed?"

"I guess I find your simplicity...refreshing."

"Simplicity?" Her grin faded. "Just because I don't put on airs and graces, it doesn't mean I can't impress your friends."

His eyes sparkled. "Oh, I have no doubt about that, sunshine, or you wouldn't be here right now with me."

She nodded. "Good." She rubbed her stomach again, too full to do anything but sleep. "When was this dress fitting thing again?" she asked. "Because I doubt anything will fit me right now."

He laughed again, and she decided she really liked the sound. She bit her bottom lip. It'd be all too easy to like this man, too. She'd need to keep her guard up and not lose herself in the fairytale of being with him.

She pushed back her chair. "If you don't mind, I'd like to have a shower and freshen up before I have any fittings."

He nodded. "You do that. I'll clean up here."

She paused. "Oh. You don't have staff to come and clean after dinner?"

He grinned wryly. "I have cleaners come in twice a week and lunch or dinners cooked for me when I request them, but mostly I keep this area of my palace to myself." He shrugged even as he stood and collected the dishes. "I don't have much privacy. I enjoy what solitude I can get."

"It's going to take a strong woman to learn to live in that spotlight with you."

He nodded, his gaze raking over her. "Indeed, it is."

Chapter Five

Amber stood on a dressmaker's platform in the large dressing room that branched off from one side of Basam's walk-in-robe. She was relieved to find the dressmaker, Marietta, had light, dexterous fingers, and the materials that were pinned around her were loose fitting and—of course—modest.

Not that it mattered. She was used to wearing a bikini so it was nothing for her to stand in her matching white panties and bra while the dressmaker clucked and fussed around her.

Amber learned Marietta had been born and lived in Paris, where she'd learned her craft before she'd been offered a position in Basam's palace. She'd apparently snapped up his offer, the salary too good to decline.

Taking out the pins from the fabric swathed around Amber, Marietta smiled as she held up yet another lovely fabric against Amber. This one was a dark mulberry color with gorgeous silver embroidery. "We call these garments, abayas. Though many women wear them as an outer garment like a cloak in traditional black, I've created these to be a little more flattering and in brighter colors."

"They're lovely," Amber conceded with a smile. "And so comfortable."

The dressmaker smiled proudly. "Feeling comfortable *and* beautiful is my goal." She nodded at the mulberry-colored one. "This will take no time to sew. I should have it ready for you in a few hours. It will be perfect for casual daywear. In the meantime, you can wear the fire-red abaya this evening."

As Marietta bagged the mulberry abaya, Amber glanced at the red creation that was on a hanger behind her. Red meant power and she had a feeling she'd need every bit of that tonight. "They're both beautiful, thank you."

Red also meant passion. Not that she'd be testing out that theory tonight or anytime soon, no matter that little thrills of delight went through her whenever Basam was in her vicinity.

Marietta smiled back. "You will be the envy of many. I'll advise the hairdresser to sweep your hair up at the sides with the back loose. A diamond tiara with matching earrings will perfectly set off your dress and hair."

Amber touched her upswept hair self-consciously. It was in its usual bun, though corkscrew strands had come loose around her face after she'd had a steaming hot shower. "That sounds lovely, but my hair is a mess of curls."

"Then you will make all the women with their straight, dark hair even more envious." She giggled like a schoolgirl. "Spiral perms will make a big comeback in this country, just you wait and see."

Amber wasn't convinced, but she was no fashionista either. She trusted in the dressmaker whose own abaya was a gorgeous, flowing creation in a rainbow of colors that swooshed and swooped around her as she worked.

Marietta's critical gaze turned satisfied. "Now that I know your measurements and have an eye for your coloring, I can make a few more creations without having to be here." She clucked her tongue, a smile creasing her face. "I have such grandiose ideas for you."

Amber ignored the sudden wilting sensation within to announce, "That is very kind of you, but I'm not sure how long I'll be—"

"Thank you, Marietta. That will be all for now," Basam interjected as he walked into the dressing room.

Amber froze even as Marietta scooped up the rest of her bags filled with fabrics and dressmaker paraphernalia and said to Basam, "She has one abaya for tonight, and another that will be ready soon. I will send the others as they're made."

He nodded. "I knew I could rely on you."

Marietta beamed. "Thank *you,* Sheikh Basam, for entrusting me."

The dressmaker hurried out the door as though her head was exploding with ideas for her new client, leaving Amber behind on a little dressmaker's platform in nothing but her panties and bra. And with nothing but Basam's hot eyes on her.

Everything inside her screamed to move, to cover up, but her legs wouldn't unlock and her eyes were caught by his as he approached, a predator ready to strike. "You are exquisite," he growled softly.

She swallowed hard at the savage intensity in his eyes and the bulge behind his thobe. He was the king of the desert now more than ever, a hunter stalking his quarry. That she was on the precipice of giving in to him caused logic to finally reinsert itself. Her muscles unlocked and she stepped down onto the carpeted floor to pick up the bathrobe and push her arms into its sleeves.

Basam chuckled indulgently. "It's too late to hide yourself from me now, sunshine. Your gorgeous body is now imprinted onto my brain."

She drew the bathrobe tighter around her. "I believe I mentioned *no* sex."

He nodded. "That you did. Though I believe I also mentioned *unless you want it.*"

She lifted her chin. "Well, I don't want it." *Liar!* She cleared her throat. "I'm here for one thing and one thing only." She grimaced at the unlikelihood of what she was about to enact. "To convince your people that we're blissfully in love."

He pushed up his thobe's sleeve and glanced at the chunky gold watch on his wrist. "Then you might want to get comfortable here for a while." He glanced around the dressing room. Beside the dressmaker's platform, there were two chairs in front of mirrors. On the counters beneath were baskets holding various makeup odds and ends. Hair products in shelves lower down sat beside straighteners and curling irons, as well as scissors and various other paraphernalia.

He glanced back at her. "The hairdresser is due to arrive shortly along with my personal jeweler."

"You have your own jeweler?"

He nodded. "Yes, he designs and handcrafts all my pieces."

She noted his thumb ring. His jeweler couldn't be too busy. She sniffed as another, unpleasant thought surfaced. "No doubt he has been kept busy making your girlfriends their pieces of jewelry?"

"Ex-girlfriends," he agreed amicably. "And those pieces were mostly parting gifts."

She arched a brow, reminded yet again of why she was here. "Is that to soften the blow of them not being the special girl who gets to marry the sheikh?"

He smirked, his dark golden eyes appraising her. "Something like that. Though, to be honest, most of them were more than happy with their consolation prize."

"Ugh, no wonder you're so cynical about women."

He cocked his head to the side. "So you're saying you're not happy with your choker and earrings or your one-hundred thousand dollar consolation prize?"

She gritted her teeth with frustration. "That's hardly the point!"

"Isn't it?" He stepped closer. "Not all the women I've been with in the past have been wealthy."

"It's nice to know you don't...discriminate," she said drily.

He sighed softly. "We're doing each other a favor." He reached out and cupped her chin, his thumb rubbing softly under her jawline and sending hot sparks straight to her core. "If we enjoy each other's company in the meantime, then all the better."

She stepped back. "All the better for *you*!"

His face flickered with emotion, too fast for her to read. "I think we both know it would be better for you, too, sunshine."

She resisted squirming at his words, all too aware he spoke the truth. She sensed with everything inside her that he was a man she wouldn't soon forget, in the bedroom and out of it. Deny it all she wanted, sex with him was becoming the focal point of her thoughts, a need that grew with every minute she spent in his company.

Her pulse fluttered. They would be sharing a bed later tonight. How was she going to resist his charismatic sexuality and chemistry? He was a force of nature, unrelenting and inescapable.

Her throat dried while other intimate places grew wet. Sooner or later she would succumb to him. It was just a matter of time.

A knock sounded at the dressing room door and Basam's mouth twisted with ironic amusement. "Saved by the bell." He spun on his heel to open the door. "That will be your hairstylist."

After he conferred with the woman, he sent Amber a little salute. "Enjoy yourself, sunshine. I'll see you in a few hours."

Chapter Six

Amber sat in her bathrobe in front of the mirror, her ocean-blue eyes widening as she watched her transformation from a frizzy-haired nobody to a stylish somebody.

Stylish enough to stand beside a sheikh?

She titled her chin. *Yes.* With her curls primped and sprayed, the sides pulled tight and pinned on top of her head beneath the sparkling tiara, she looked like a princess.

It turned out the hairstylist, Nasira, was also a makeup artist. Though Amber said she wanted a natural look, she blinked and stared at the woman staring back who looked like a movie star with her kohl-lined eyes, white sparkling eyelids and blood-red lips.

Nasira smiled as she stepped behind her to admire Amber's reflection. "You will be a sensation tonight." She stroked a hand through the back of Amber's hair, pulling the curls straight. "Your hair is beautiful. If it was straightened, it would fall below your waist."

"No. Don't straighten it." Amber jumped a little at Basam's husky voice, his stare then sweeping over her as though she was a goddess. She shivered. If she hadn't felt like a goddess before, she most certainly did now. His eyes worshipped her. *"Never* straighten it," he added before he stood behind her and touched one of the bouncy strands. His gaze held hers in the mirror. "Your hair is perfect."

Something shifted inside her chest. She'd always been self-conscious about her wild, untamed hair, but Basam's admiration made all her insecurities melt clean away. "Thank you."

"I agree," Nasira said with a wide smile, her eyes moving from Basam to Amber and back to Basam again. She looked at the fire-red abaya hanging behind them. "I'll help her to dress before I go."

"I'll help her to put it on." Nasira blinked in shock, and he added coolly, "Thank you, Nasira."

She bowed slightly, gathered up the few things she'd brought with her, then hurried out of the dressing room.

Amber was caught somewhere between relief they were alone and anger that her name would be dragged through the mud the moment Nasira flapped her gums about the inappropriate behavior between Basam and his western girlfriend.

"You look upset," he murmured, his big hands clasping her robe-clad shoulders.

"Then you'd be right."

"Oh?"

"I don't want your people to think I'm just another crass western woman with loose morals and no self-respect."

"You care what my people think?" he murmured, sounding surprised.

Her eyes flashed blue fire at him in the mirror. "If I'm to come out of this charade unscathed, then yes, I do care."

He nodded. "You're right. We need to preserve your good name." He cocked his head to the side, his eyes holding hers in the mirror. "Is there anything from your past I should know about, gossip that might find its way over here? Our newspapers can be very...thorough."

She squeezed her eyes closed, her heart thumping dully in her ears. *Shit.* She hadn't considered her past being brought into question. But surely not even the most astute reporter would uncover her family's darkest secrets. That she alone seemed unscathed by addictive needs that hadn't quite gotten past her brother, thanks to his gambling, would mean little to the press.

A good story was a good story as far as they would be concerned.

"Amber?" he prompted.

She shook her head, her eyes opening. "No. Nothing," she lied.

His gaze seemed to read deep into her own and she looked away, needing to find relief from the silent cross-examination of his stare.

"In that case...let's get you dressed. My people are impatiently waiting for the woman I call my girlfriend."

She inhaled a steadying breath, then nodded and stood before she disrobed. When he in turn sucked in a breath, she was glad of her toned and tanned body. She had never be an office girl type of woman, she loved the joy of riding waves and being outside in the sun and salt air, staying fit and active.

Being a girlfriend to a sheikh was way out of her comfort zone. She was no actor. She wasn't even a half-decent waitress let alone someone who'd fool an entire nation into believing she was worthy of their sheikh.

Basam withdrew the red abaya from its hangar. "Arms up," he instructed.

She lifted them obediently, the silky fabric then sliding over her body, the hem settling at her ankles. She touched the tiny little spray of silver gems embedded into its bodice.

"Diamonds," he murmured with a smile. "They'll go perfectly with your tiara and the choker and earrings I gifted you."

She nodded. "I left them on the vanity in the bathroom. I didn't want to get them wet," she admitted.

His smile was wide as he escorted her to the bathroom. "You might be the first girl I've met who appreciates the value of diamonds."

She shrugged weakly. "They don't grow on trees, at least, not where I'm from."

He chuckled. "Believe me, they don't here, either. My currency here is oil."

"Black gold?" she asked.

"More or less. Not that it's my only income stream. I have...many."

She stood on the white tiles with gold accents, her eyes meeting Basam's in the vanity mirror as he lifted the choker and brought it to her throat. She swallowed hard as his fingertips touched her flesh, tingles cascading right through her body at the contact.

It wasn't until he secured the choker that she clipped in the earrings, then stared at her reflection. "Is that really me?"

"You're stunning," he said hoarsely, his hands dropping from her throat to her shoulders.

"Thank you," she said huskily. She looked up...and up. He towered over her, her head just reaching the top of his shoulders. "You don't look half-bad yourself." His white thobe and keffiyeh with matching gold edging was striking. She cleared her throat. "But I should probably put on my heeled sandals so I don't look pint-sized next to you."

Though to be fair, most people would probably look small beside him.

Her heels clacked on the shiny marble floor in white and cream swirled with gold as she walked beside her sheikh "boyfriend" through a dozen different corridors, until one opened into a huge room where a string quartet played to guests who socialized below crystal chandeliers. Stone pillars supported a floor above, where shiny gold balustrades showcased a viewing platform, a few dozen guests peering down at everyone else.

Wait-staff hurried between the crowd and a curved, polished cedar bar at one end of the room, their trays stacked with flutes of champagne, fancy cocktails and boutique beers.

She hid a smile. That had been her just a few days ago; balancing flutes of champagne on a tray...until she'd spilled the expensive bubbly everywhere. No, not just anywhere. She'd had the humiliation of spilling it all over the sheikh.

And now look at me...living the Cinderella fairytale that is every girl's dream.

A hush descended when the guests noticed their sheikh and Amber arrive, and she felt the blood drain from her face at the sudden attention from so many aristocratic people. She could all but smell the wealth in the room, the glittering jewels at the women's throats and wrists and earlobes, the gold chunky watches at the men's wrists. The people who'd been guests of Basam's at the Queensland island had been little more than peasants in comparison.

She clung onto him, drawing from his strength when she was so far out of her depth she was all but drowning.

"Remember, you're one of us now," he murmured. "You already look the part. Now you just have to act it."

He drew her closer to his side as a group of five men and two women approached. It turned out they were dignitaries whose names went in one ear and out the other. But her confidence grew as they moved from one group to another, the conversation flowing more naturally.

The story she shared with Basam was easy enough to maintain, considering it was based on truth. They'd met at a party where she'd been waitressing. Her flutes of champagne had fallen on him and their eyes had connected, their instant chemistry the start of something neither of them could deny.

The latter might have been a stretch, but a part of her couldn't deny the attraction, at least on her side, had been real.

Basam stroked his thumb over her inner wrist as he retold the same story yet again to another small but avid audience, her throat drying and her heart rate surging. His touch might be a small gesture, but it was a blatantly possessive one, one that made her wish for things that could never be.

They were heading toward yet another group of guests when an older man and a young, beautiful woman approached, intercepting them. The young woman's dark eyes flashed with emotion, her even darker hair that fell to her waist carefully intertwined with jewels that sparkled under the light of the many chandeliers.

"Sheikh Basam," the older man greeted.

"Amal," Basam said in return, then glanced at the young woman and said, "Maram, how lovely to see you."

Amber sucked in a breath at the name she instantly recognized even as Maram inclined her head, as regal as any princess and ten times more beautiful.

This was the woman Basam wasn't attracted to and didn't want to marry?

Was he for real?

Maram was exquisite.

The woman turned her liquid dark eyes Amber's way, a gleam of something hostile for a moment showing itself before her shields went up and she smiled sweetly. "You must be Amber. I've heard so much about you."

"News travels fast," Amber murmured.

"It certainly does," Maram said with a husky voice. "But not as fast as the rate you two apparently fell in love."

Apparently?

Basam put his arm around Amber and drew her closer. "I was never a believer in love at first sight, until it happened to me. Now I can't help but wonder if it was fate that conspired to push us together."

Amber blinked at him. "Fate has the weirdest sense of humor for me to have to spill drinks on you to get my attention."

"I was aware of you long before the drinks scenario," he said throatily, his arm moving up and down her back in an intimate caress. "I just used the accident as an excuse to get to know you better."

Amber ignored the electricity of his touch as she gazed adoringly up at him while he said the sweet words of nothing, which really *were* sweet words of nothing. She only hoped her acting was as strong as the yearning that filled her from the inside out. What would it be like to have something like Basam *really* fall in love with her?

A man who could have any woman he wanted. A man so good looking and powerful—and not just because of his wealth, he carried himself with a confidence that was mesmerizing—it was like standing near the sun and becoming part of his radiance.

"If only I'd known being clumsy could be such an attractive trait perhaps I would have spilled something on you too?" Maram said sweetly, but with such venomous undertones her father cleared his throat and shuffled his feet.

"Now, now, Maram. I'm sure *your* Mr. Right will sweep you off your feet when you least expect it."

"Perhaps he'll have to mop around my feet instead?"

Her father winced, then turned narrowed eyes back to Basam. "I hope you know what you're doing, Sheikh Basam. You could have had everything."

"I *do* have everything," Basam said evenly, his voice as neutral as his expression.

Maram's fists clenched by her sides. "Wait until the real Amber is exposed," she said icily. As she walked away with her father, she said over a shoulder, "Don't say I didn't warn you."

Amber frowned. "Well that was pleasant." *Not.* She looked at Basam. "And what does she mean by exposing the real Amber?"

Basam sighed. "Maram's family owns a publishing house, which includes a major newspaper. My guess is she'll use one of the reporters to dig a little into your past and try to expose anything she can find about you."

Amber gaped, her insides freezing. "She can't do that, can she?"

"She might be full of hot air and grievances," he conceded, her tension easing the smallest bit. "But knowing Maram," he added, "she'll go through with her threat and try to find anything she can on you to discredit our relationship."

Amber's tension returned full force and Basam clasped her hand in his and drew her toward the bar. "I think a drink might be in order."

Chapter Seven

Amber had never been much of a drinker, she refused to touch the stuff most of the time, but she needed something strong after the brief but unpleasant meeting with the woman Basam didn't want as his wife.

She accepted the date liquor and gulped it down, enjoying the way it burned all the way down her throat.

"Would you like another?" Basam asked.

She nodded. "Please."

She was a little giddy by the time she'd swallowed down the second drink, but it made whatever nerves she'd had disappear as if they'd never been. She could handle being the sheikh's girlfriend! She could handle anything that came her way!

She put her empty glass on the bar, spinning back around as the string quartet stopped playing and exotic music suddenly rang out from speakers hidden inside the palace walls. Two rows of women in tiny beaded tops and bared midriffs with jeweled pants then entered the room in formation.

Amber cheered when she realized the women would be tonight's entertainment. The dancers lifted their arms in unison, their strong midriffs rippling as they undulated to the music, music tinkling from their hands as they clacked their fingers together.

"They're using zils—finger cymbals," he informed her as he watched her watch the dancers. "I usually also have live musicians to accompany the dancers."

"I wish you had," she said, her body swaying to the seductive music along with the dancers. "I would have loved to have seen this in all its authentic glory."

"Perhaps another night," he murmured close behind her, his arms encircling her waist from behind as he pulled her against him.

She stiffened, her eyes darting around the room. This wouldn't be considered appropriate behavior in this country, would it? But everyone was staring at the performance, not at them, and she relaxed against him, enjoying his strong front against her back.

Perhaps sheikhs were given more free rein than others? Or perhaps his country was more forward thinking than many others in that respect?

The hairs on the back of her neck stood up and her eyes automatically lifted, finding the burning stare of Maram who watched them together. Amber managed a smile but the other woman looked away, then disappeared through the crowd and out of sight.

She sighed. It seemed she'd made an enemy here without even trying. Luckily she was getting paid well to fool everyone. Basam was just as unavailable as he always was and it had nothing to do with her, despite the ruse they acted out.

The dancers moved through the crowd then, their fingers clanging out sweet notes on their zils as they lifted their arms and swayed their hips suggestively. When one particularly lovely lady approached Basam and danced in front of him, Amber's stomach clenched while acid burned its way through her body.

What's wrong with me? He's not my real boyfriend, he never will be! I'm nothing to him—just as he's nothing to me!

Yet the burn remained long after the dancer left him alone. That he'd barely taken his eyes off Amber the whole time didn't make her feel any better. He was acting the part for the audience watching, nothing more.

Only once the dancers finished their performance and left the room the same way they'd come to cheers and applause, did Basam lean close to her and murmur, "Ready to call it a night, sunshine?"

She nodded, the clench in her stomach moving down to her core.

She swallowed hard. Calling it a night didn't automatically mean he wanted to seduce her...did it? She'd told him "no sex" and he seemed a man of his word. That her body and mind fought a battle over whether she wanted sex now was another matter entirely.

Her thoughts continued traveling a dangerous path as Basam stepped forward, his clear, strong voice encompassing the room. "Thank you, ladies and gentleman for coming here tonight and making my lovely girlfriend, Amber—or sunshine, as I like to call her—so very welcome." A smattering of laughter sounded. "I feel very fortunate to have found a woman who's become so precious to me in such a short time."

More of the audience clapped and sighed, and Amber managed a smile even as a camera flashed and the photographer strode forward to take more shots.

Basam nodded and stepped back beside Amber. Bending close to her ear, he said softly, "Did I mention the official photos that would be taken tonight?"

"No, it seems to have slipped your mind," she sniped under her breath.

He turned and caught her chin in one big hand, his eyes glinting then as he lowered his mouth to hers and stole a kiss that, though brief, made her knees knock together while passion sparked deep inside. He drew back, his lips twitching. "Looks like I've found a way to make your eyes less flashy and hostile and more passionate and dewy."

She blinked up at him even as he caught her closer and smiled like the wolf that had cornered a doe while the cameraman took at least dozen more shots. Only once Basam was satisfied there were enough shots did he incline his head and escort Amber toward the exit, his guests watching them depart.

"Are you okay?" he asked as they traversed the wide corridors, where paintings and prints were interspersed with what appeared to be centuries-old needlework in huge, gold-leaf frames.

She nodded. "I think so." She looked up at him, admiring his dark hair and high cheekbones, his full lips that had mastered hers so effectively. "Did I pass the test?"

He smiled and nodded. "We were very convincing."

A delicate shiver went down her spine. "Maram certainly seemed to believe us." She bit her bottom lip. "I think I understand now why you don't want to marry her, she's very—"

Hostile. Vindictive. Mean.

"Possessive?" he asked, filling in the blank.

"Something like that."

"Unfortunately she's as much in love with the idea of being sheikha as she'll ever be in love with me."

"So what do *you* want in a woman?" Amber asked. "It clearly isn't someone who is beautiful and self-assured or you'd at least test the waters with Maram."

"No, I've met plenty of other beautiful and self-assured women. Unfortunately, not all of them have other qualities I'm also attracted to."

"Such as?"

"Such as compassion, kindness, loyalty and honor."

"It sounds like you're after perfection," she said with a sniff, though a part of her was impressed he sought beauty that wasn't just skin deep. "None of us are perfect, we all come with flaws."

"Some more than others," he mused.

"And what about *your* imperfections?" she asked. "Do the women have any say about those?"

He shrugged. "I have plenty, but I work on my failings and I'd never force anyone to marry me. I'd like to think the woman I end up with will see the good inside me, the good I hope to extend to my people, my country."

The burn inside her body made its way to her chest. She envied the woman who'd turn this man's head. She'd be one lucky lady, someone Basam would love without reserve and protect with his life.

"Then I hope you find her," she finally said. If only she could decipher the long look he sent her as they stepped into his suite of rooms.

Chapter Eight

"Drink?" Basam asked as Amber followed him inside.

She shook her head. "Thank you, but no. I think I've had enough for the night."

He nodded and poured himself one. "Feel free to take a shower while I indulge." His smile was a little crooked. "I might need two or three more yet to numb the images in my head."

"Images?"

He nodded. "Yes. Ones that include you standing naked with water running over your body."

Hadn't she had those exact same thoughts herself while he'd showered in the bathroom of his private jet? Not that she'd be telling him that anytime soon. It was bad enough she had a pulse pounding in her ears and between her thighs.

She washed and dried herself in record time, dressing into a lacy white nightgown that she'd packed for the island motel. Though it was modest by her usual standards, looking in the mirror it suddenly seemed too short, the bodice dipping too low.

Her face heating, she slipped back into the bedroom and climbed under the covers of the huge bed before Basam put in an appearance. With any luck she'd be asleep before he joined her.

So why did heat build between her legs at the thought of his big body spooning hers? His arousal straining against her...

Ugh. This was barely night two and already she was fantasizing about the man—the sheikh—who'd hired her because he'd believed there was no chance she'd want more from him than money. If he knew how much more she really did want from him, he'd send her packing on the first plane back home.

Or perhaps he'd be in bed with her right now, his big body surging inside her, his heat turning her into a furnace before she combusted with pleasure.

She sighed heavily. She'd never really fantasized about anyone before, had never really believed in lust at first sight. She was quickly changing her mindset. At least she wouldn't have to pretend to be attracted to him. Her every cell came to life whenever he was near, his body a magnet for her own.

She rolled one way, then the other, restless and wide awake. There was no way she'd sleep tonight. Not in a million years.

Yet one second she was lying on Basam's bed, the next she was standing at the cemetery beside her brother, her eyes burning but dry while her brother quietly sobbed as clods of dirt landed on their parents' coffins at the bottom of the hole.

Amber's hands squeezed into fists at her sides as the loamy earth scent filled the air, reminding her just how fragile life was. Yet resentment and anger festered inside her right along with grief and despair. Her mom and dad should never have left her and Zach behind, but their parents had been selfish and neglectful, and too wrapped up in their own needs to worry about their children's wellbeing.

Everything blurred for a second, and suddenly she was standing in front of her brother, their surrounds a weird kaleidoscope of colors as she handed him a wad of cash—a hundred-thousand to be exact—money she'd earned in seven days doing Basam's bidding.

It had all been worth it though just to see Zach's eyes fill with even more tears, these ones of gratitude and thanks as the weight of debt lifted off his shoulders, setting him free—setting them both free.

She smiled at him, her heart overflowing. "Just promise me you will use every last dollar to pay off your debts. No more gambling, Zach."

"You have my word," he vowed.

The kaleidoscope of colors swirled, and she immediately knew months had flown by as she stood in a gray pantsuit in a crowd of colorfully dressed people. *Where am I?* Wherever she was, nobody seemed to notice her, and she certainly didn't taken too much notice of them, she was too busy focusing on her brother as she picked him out far ahead, striding through the bright mass of people.

The anxiety she'd barely withheld suddenly escalated as she sensed Zach's resolve. He was on a mission and no one was going to stop him. She hurried after him as he pushed and shoved his way through the men in their suits and women in their frocks and hats, some with fascinators.

Her heart kicked into double beats as realization hit her and she paused before she did a full turn. A long, green racetrack took up a large circumference below her, grandstands and grassy viewing areas flowing around it, along with buildings for corporate seating, restaurants and sports betting.

Five or six horses were being led out into the parade area, where punters craned their necks to take a good, hard look at what they deemed was the next winning steed.

Her vision blurred. Zach was here getting his fix. He wasn't worried about the debts he owed; not right now. He wanted the rush of winning that gambling gave him. He wanted to swim in the cash he imagined he'd secure.

Rage filled. How dare he! She'd trusted him! She'd sacrificed a week of her life to pay for debts he owed while erecting a wall over her heart so that she wouldn't fall for the damn sheikh. She'd done everything to ensure her brother wouldn't lose his wife, his daughter!

"Zach, no!" she screamed.

Every single head in the crowd turned her way except her brother's.

She woke with a sharp inhalation, sitting up in bed with her breathing choppy and her chest heaving. There was enough light from under the bathroom door to reveal she was no longer in bed alone.

She cranked her head around slowly, allowing her vision to slowly filter in the long length of Basam under the covers as he lay in bed with her, his hands behind his head, his eyes open and alert.

Her voice came out as a croak. "You're awake."

He nodded. "Yes. You were deep asleep when I came to bed. Not that you were exactly having a restful slumber."

Her mouth dried. "Oh?"

His eyes held hers, and even in the dim room his gaze was assessing. "Who is Zach?"

"What does it matter?" she asked wearily.

"It matters a lot," he said softly, but with such undertones of intent it took everything she had not to flinch. He was like a starved dog with a meaty bone, and she was the bone that no one else was allowed near.

Not because he had feelings for her, far from it. His possessive nature stemmed from the fact he'd paid her for seven days, a role that required her complete devotion...to him.

She closed her eyes briefly, but it didn't stop the pain of betrayal from crowding in on her. "Zach is my brother," she said.

Basam touched her spine with one hand, then stroked up and down. But it didn't ease her tension, if anything his touch escalated it. She was a live wire stretched to breaking point and he was the weight fraying it faster.

"Tell me about him," Basam said gently. "What did he do to make you sound so distraught?"

She pushed the heel of her hand against her brow, wishing she could just fall back to sleep and pretend the dream never happened, along with this conversation. Pretend that her past was just that—her past. But being in denial hadn't helped Zach and it certainly wasn't helping her.

"Zach was nineteen and I was seventeen—five years ago now—when we lost both our parents in a car crash." Basam continued stroking up and down her spine, but he didn't interrupt, just waited patiently for her to continue. Her breath shuddered out. "At that time we had no one but each other, except although Zach did his best to fill the void of our parents' death, he never got over his grief."

She didn't realize she was crying until she touched her face and it was wet, like she'd opened up floodgates and didn't know how to shut them again. Perhaps neither of them had yet gotten over it. She cleared her throat. "Zach was always searching for escape. One day he went with a friend to the races and placed a small bet with big odds."

"I'm guessing he won?" Basam asked.

"Yes, unfortunately, he did. He won a few thousand. I-I think that was just the beginning of his addiction to gambling and to feeling good. Gambling was what filled the void, even if for a short time."

"Has your brother gotten his gambling under control now?"

She huffed out a breath. "I wish I could say yes, but no, he hasn't. Despite all his best intentions he can't seem to overcome it."

She bowed her head, wishing things were different, better. If Zach couldn't get a hold of his gambling problem, his wife and daughter would leave him, whether his debts were paid off or not. Amber didn't want to think about what he might do without them in his life.

"You mentioned at the time having no one else but each other. Is there someone in your life now?" he asked.

She shook her head. "No."

He didn't need to know that the few men she'd been with had been absolute duds in the bedroom and she hadn't cared to repeat the experience. She had a feeling being with Basam sexually would ruin any future relationships as no other man would compare. Even more reason not to become intimate with him.

"Good," he said starkly. "I'd hate for any newspapers to uncover a boyfriend I didn't know about while you're meant to be with me."

"It would complicate things a little," she agreed.

His hand moved from her spine to her upper arm. "You're still a little tense. You should be sleeping like a baby right now."

"Except I'm not a baby."

"Don't I know it," he muttered, even as she lay back down with him, doing her best not to notice his...maleness as her head rested on his shoulder like a pillow.

Despite their chemistry, she trusted him, trusted his vow not to have sex with her unless she wanted it. That she *did* want it wasn't something he needed to know, especially when, oddly enough, she began to relax.

"So tell me about your family," she said drowsily.

"There's not much to tell," he said huskily. "Like you, I lost my parents too young. They died within months of each other, my mother from cancer and my dad from a broken heart, although I was told it was ultimately from a stroke. Unlike you though, I'm an only child."

"I couldn't imagine how hard it must have been going through your grief all alone."

He swiped a hand over his bristles. "I wasn't totally alone. Amal became something of a mentor for me while I mourned for my parents while learning how to run my country. The fact I listened to him above my own advisors spoke volumes. I trusted in him completely."

"What changed?"

He blew out a slow, thoughtful breath. "I think he assumed it was a natural progression to go from being his mentor to having him as a father-in-law, and since his daughter is considered beautiful by many, I guess he never vouched for any objections from me at the idea."

"Does he not realize her beauty is only skin-deep?"

Basam laughed. "She could look like a goat and I'm sure he'd adore her, as any father should. As for her personality, he sees only the best in her."

"What about you?"

"I worked her out a long time ago."

"Were you ever...intimate with her?"

His shoulder flexed a little under her head when he asked, "Would it bother you if I had been?"

Would it bother him if it *did* bother her? She lifted her chin. "Of course not. You're paying me to do a job, it matters little to me if you've screwed her or half your kingdom, for that matter."

"Liar," he said huskily.

She frowned, her face heating. "Why do you say that?"

"If it didn't bother you there would be no tension returning to your body and your voice wouldn't rise an octave."

"What are you, a psychologist now?"

"I know how to read body language," he murmured. "It's a trait I've not only been trained to uncover, but learned over the years with my many negotiations and meetings."

She turned to him them, her body thrumming with arousal as his unique scent of spiced amber filled her senses. "What's my body language telling you now?"

His eyes flashed, then narrowed. "It's telling me you want me to roll you underneath me and kiss you and make out, then take charge of your body by claiming you completely, filling you with—"

"I think I get it," she cut in hoarsely.

"All you have to do is say the word," he said evenly.

It took everything she had to shake her head. "No. I don't want to develop feelings for you." Ones that would never be returned. She rolled away from him to her side of the bed and shut her eyes, but not before hearing his heavy, regretful sigh.

Chapter Nine

The aroma of coffee woke Amber from a sleep muddled with dreams about her parents. She sighed heavily. Sometimes those dreams when she remembered the days when her mom and dad had been fun and caring hurt more than the horrid nightmares about them.

She stretched a little, but didn't need to reach out to know Basam wasn't there. It was more than a little unnerving that every cell in her body instinctively knew when he was absent.

She grimaced. She'd need her caffeine fix today.

She'd taken this job offer, not only for the money, but in the knowledge she wouldn't get romantically involved or attached.

How's that working out for you so far?

If night two had seen her close to succumbing to sex, how close would she get tonight? She sat and swung out of bed, padding barefooted across the thick cream carpet and out into the dining and lounge room, following the coffee beans aroma to where a coffee machine sat proudly on one side of Basam's huge mahogany bar.

Not that she was really focused on anything other than the bare-chested man who was a vision for her eyes.

"You're awake," he said with a smile, his loose white pants, which most men wore under their thobes, sitting low on his hips and showcasing rippling abs along with a faint line of dark hair that started just below his navel and disappeared beneath his pants waistband. "And just in time for a coffee," he added.

She blinked at him, her mouth drying while other, far more intimate parts of her body flooded with liquid heat. She pulled her stare away from him to focus on the fully automated coffee machine. "I didn't realize until now that you don't have a kitchen."

She'd clearly been distracted.

"No need for one when I have amazing chefs cooking for me. But I do enjoy having coffee at my fingertips." He nodded at the machine. "Milk or sugar?"

"Milk, no sugar," she said.

Not even a minute later she was sipping on possibly the best coffee she'd ever tasted. They mightn't have fabulous beaches here—*any* beaches—but they certainly knew how to make a damn good beverage.

He made another coffee, then took intermittent mouthfuls of it between speaking. "Enjoy your coffee in peace while you can." At her arched eyebrow he explained, "We'll be sharing breakfast this morning in the dining hall with some of last night's guests."

She gulped down the last of her coffee. "No two guesses who some of those guests might be," she said.

He nodded. "Despite our differences, Amal is still a very dear friend of mine."

She bit her bottom lip, then acknowledged, "It's kind of endearing that you don't walk away from a close friendship simply because you don't desire his daughter."

Not in marriage, anyway.

His lips quirked. "I'm not sure Amal or Maram find it particularly endearing.

She shrugged. "Maram is beautiful, I don't doubt for a second that some gorgeous man will sweep her off her feet."

Basam grinned ruefully. "I'm sure she will, too, just as long as she doesn't show her true colors."

He placed his empty coffee cup on the bar. "My staff will take our dirty dishes away." He nodded toward the bedroom. "We'd best get dressed for our breakfast get-together."

Get-together? Her stomach crunched. She hadn't expected to have to face anyone first thing in the morning and hadn't prepared herself for any further interrogation from people she didn't know.

He smiled at her. "Don't look so worried. The dressmaker has already dropped off a couple more abayas for you to choose from, as well as some shoes and accessories.

She might always love the less-is-more wardrobe, but she was getting to love the loose and flowing abayas that covered up the body and yet made her feel utterly beautiful. She entered the dining hall with Basam, half-expecting some huge room with scarred wooden tables and some Vikings tearing at pheasant legs and charred pork.

The only thing she'd gotten right was the huge room. Except this one had a trio of matching crystal chandeliers hanging from the high ceiling that spread soft, glowing light onto three eighteen-seater tables covered in fine white cloths.

Only the closest table was being used, with the entire breakfast party seated except for two empty cushioned chairs at one end. They were clearly for the sheikh and his guest, AKA pretend girlfriend.

Amber felt Maram's eyes on her and the gorgeous mulberry abaya she wore with its glistening silver thread and matching silver heels. She'd piled her blonde hair on top her head in a knot that mostly restrained it with just a few tendrils falling free either side of her face. She'd also put on a very light makeup, nothing more than peach lipstick and mascara.

Maram's gaze moved to instead soak in Basam. Who wouldn't? He looked every inch the powerful and commanding sheikh in his white thobes and Keffiyeh headdress, his very presence compelling and magnetic.

Basam pulled a chair out for Amber, then waited until she was seated before he took the one next to her and looked around. "Thank you all for waiting. I trust none of you are yet starving?"

A handful of his guests chuckled—they'd eaten and drank like kings last night—while a few more smiled and stayed respectfully silent. Only an elderly man muttered, "We're more than happy to wait," as he adjusted his keffiyeh with shaky, gnarled hands.

"Then let's eat!" Basam announced. And though there were already platters on the table that included glistening melons and grapes, and plates with dates, figs and a diverse selection of camel and goat's cheese, his servants began carrying out steaming hot food before placing them in the center of the table.

Amber ate some falafel followed by a round of pita bread that she pushed into a dip of cooked and mashed fava beans, adding a little splash of olive oil for good measure. She couldn't resist then adding some of the fruit and cheese to her plate. It was all so delicious.

Everyone was replete when the team of servants reappeared and began clearing away the dirty dishes and remaining food. Then a young lad brought a tray out with newspapers on top. He immediately headed toward Basam and set down the newspapers, bowing his head a little before retreating from the room.

Basam smiled. "My favorite time of day. Finding out what is going on in my country and the rest of the world."

"You might be surprised," Maram muttered.

Amber glanced at the first newspaper's headline. That it showcased a picture of Basam with her in the doorway of his private jet where they were kissing caused her breath to punch out of her lungs even before she read the text underneath.

Basam and his new girlfriend have yet to touch the ground as sparks fly between them.

The next paper's photo showcased them at the party where he'd introduced her to his friends. In this one they'd just kissed, his hand under her chin with their eyes locked with intense emotion.

Could this western girlfriend finally be 'the one' for Sheikh Basam?

He looked up at her with a smile. "You must have made a great first impression, sunshine. Usually the press is much more underhanded and scathing. But thanks to your graciousness, they've embraced you."

She blinked. "I was just being myself."

"Exactly. You're an anomaly to them. Not only were you being polite by introducing yourself after disembarking from the jet, you didn't hide your face and avoid the reporters, or contrarily strut past them like you were on a catwalk. You were natural, and it was clearly appreciated."

He shuffled the newspapers, reading the headline of the last one. Amber blinked again, her stomach knotting and throat tightening as the words hit her like a punch to the solar plexus.

Meet Basam's mystery girlfriend. Who is she and what secrets does she hide?

Amber instantly knew the last headline was from Maram's publisher. They'd planted the seed of suspicion. They'd dig deep now to find whatever they could to feed their readership every crumb of information and gossip possible.

It would only be a matter of time before the articles discussed their sheikh being with a commoner. She only hoped the reporters of this newspaper didn't get too unscrupulous with their research.

Maram looked at her with glittering eyes. "You look...appalled, as though you popped a piece of lemon in your mouth after imagining you'd gotten the cherry on top," she said with a light, teasing laugh that barely concealed her callous undercurrents.

The rest of the guests sucked in shocked breaths, but Amber knew she couldn't make a scene in return. She had to be the dignified, grown-up one. She smiled sweetly at the woman. "Not at all. It's more how exposed I feel knowing the public has seen our love for one another." She shrugged and said demurely, "I'm a very...private person."

Maram's malicious smile faded while the other guests *oohed* and *ahhed* at seeing such love. If only they knew the truth and that the love they imagined was just that—imagined. Fake. A con of the highest order. Her heart ached even before Basam picked up her hand, then pressed a kiss to her knuckles, his stare not once leaving hers.

"You've shown me the true meaning of love, sunshine. I couldn't be more grateful for you spilling champagne on my favorite suit."

More laughs sounded, and Amber was all too aware of the spike of wishful thinking inside her while Maram's spiteful glare cut through the love-filled atmosphere like a sharpened blade.

Chapter Ten

Amber was grateful for the time alone she had after breakfast, where she sat in Basam's sitting room reading a science fiction book she'd found on one of the shelves in the room. That she also missed the man who'd hired her to be his pretend girlfriend was something she was trying to ignore. She would *not* go there. Nothing else mattered other than the job she'd been paid to do.

That he'd had talks with his advisors and some of the guests who were staying for a few more days meant she wasn't the only one with a job to do. Not only did he have to fulfill his role as sheikh, he also had to act his part as her smitten lover.

A pity he'd never see her as more than some attractive woman on his payroll. She winced at the twinge that went straight through her chest, then set her book down with a heavy sigh. Who was she kidding? Not even a great read was going to get her out of her own thoughts today. But perhaps a swim would? Water activities always put her in a good mood.

With the lap pool private and no one around to be offended at seeing her half-naked, she pulled on a champagne-colored bikini from the walk-in closet, already feeling better in what was her everyday wear back home. Grabbing a towel, she pushed open the door at the far end of his suite of rooms, then entered the lap pool enclosure. The water glistening beckoningly, tinted skylights letting in the sunlight without its heat.

Dropping her towel onto the nearest sun lounge, she dived into the aquamarine pool. The cool water slid over her in a luxurious rush. She tilted her head back, her momentum gliding her to the surface of the water before she kicked her legs and freestyled to the other end of the pool.

She'd been swimming for almost an hour by the time she glided to one end of the pool and stayed there while she caught her breath.

Exercise really was the best therapy. She'd needed this swim, needed to feel water wrapped around her again even if it was without the salt content she loved.

The back of her neck prickling, she turned her head sharply, exhaling in a rush at seeing Basam sitting on one of the many chairs around the pool. "How long have you been sitting there?"

"Long enough to admire your stamina and grace in the water."

"Thank you. Though to be fair, water has been a part of my life since before I could walk." She cocked a brow, mentally disrobing him of his thobe and keffiyeh headgear. "You're not joining me?"

"Not right now. Our guests are waiting for us."

She blinked water out of her eyes, then swam to the edge of the pool toward the steps. "You should have told me sooner!"

His eyes darkened as she climbed out of the pool, water sliding off her even as some beads stubbornly clung on. She bent and grabbed her towel from the sun lounge and began to dry off.

"No need, they can wait," he said huskily. His stare caught and held hers. "I'm sure they'd understand and indulge my desire to see my girlfriend doing what she loves best."

She wrapped the towel around torso, ignoring a sudden shiver that wasn't from any chill in the air. Longing poured through her and, for just a handful of seconds, she allowed herself to imagine he was being real and that she was his girlfriend in every way, a woman who held his attention.

She shook off the impossible dream and managed a smile as her bare feet slapped across the mosaic pavers to where he sat. She tilted her head to the side. "What exactly are these guests waiting to do?"

He pushed to his feet. "Let's just say it's an outdoor activity, one I organized so that you might enjoy your stay here a little more."

She didn't bother telling him that her stay was far from boring already when he filled her thoughts and her fantasies day and night. She took off her towel and used it to squeeze out the excess moisture from her frizzy, tied-back hair.

Big mistake.

He sucked in a sharp breath, his gaze drinking in her half-naked body before he lifted his eyes, their stares colliding. Growling low in his throat, he pushed to his feet and reached for her, drawing her close. His head swooped and their mouths fused, and the world seemingly closed in until it was just the two of them existing.

Her moan mingled with his passion-filled growl. They might have kissed before but it'd been nothing compared to this private moment, with no one watching their every move. Desire burned through her, igniting a fuse deep inside her, an explosion just waiting to lay her bare and open her up to the very man she'd promised to keep her distance from romantically.

When he finally drew back, his dark eyes were glowing with glints of amber and ocher, his voice raspy when he finally spoke. "I've wanted to do that all day, sunshine."

She gulped back a sudden need to admit her own failings about wanting to kiss him...and more. But he hadn't hired her for that, in fact he'd expressly hired her for the very opposite reason. He wanted someone who'd walk away unscathed after their week-long pretense, and that was what she intended to do.

An hour later she walked out the back of the palace with him, to where ten other guests waited, including Maram, though her father was noticeably absent. A fenced-in yard showcased a number of camels, while eleven more were sitting on the parched ground in their saddles and halters with attached lead ropes.

Amber giggled. "At least now I understand why you told me to wear pants underneath my abaya along with closed-in shoes."

He'd also advised her to wear something light, so she'd chosen a pale blue, cotton abaya. That she'd matched it with a colorful hijab somehow worked together. She liked the point of difference.

He nodded. "I don't want you suffering from chafe marks and bruising."

She hid a pleased smile at his thoughtfulness. He might have servants running around doing his bidding and people bowing and scraping to be noticed by him, but it didn't stop him from caring about others. He was without question a great sheikh.

The sun was burning those parts of her bared to the sun—her hands and her face. She touched her colorful hijab. It already protected her head, but she could no doubt use it to cover all her face, except for her eyes, from any further burn or if the wind picked up and blew sand around.

She looked at the row of camels once again. "Which camel is mine?"

He nodded to the first one that was a light golden-brown color. "You'll be riding with me, the rest will follow behind."

She realized then that the first camel was the only one with a double saddle. No wonder there were eleven camels to twelve riders! Anticipation burbled through her, along with a little fear. "Just letting you know this will be my first time riding a camel."

He chuckled. "I figured as much, which is why I also figured you'd enjoy it a whole lot more with a rider in front of you."

A servant led two more camels out of the yard. They were loaded up with baskets and blankets and other supplies.

Basam nodded at them. "Our pack camels will follow at the very back." He looked at her. "Each one of them are very well trained animals, you have nothing to worry about."

She nodded and smiled. "Thank you. I trust you."

His stare darkened, his voice lowering. "That's good to know, sunshine."

"I'd hate to interrupt, but what time do you expect we'll be leaving?" Maram asked, her voice sharp.

Basam's eyes narrowed a little, before he turned to the rest of the group and called out. "If everyone else is ready, choose a camel behind the first one and mount up."

Everyone hurried to their camel of choice, and Maram was left with no option but to mount the very last saddled camel, the pack-camels right behind her. With her white abaya and its lace trim, along with her matching hijab, she'd probably look more sandy-yellow than pristine-white by the end of the ride.

Basam clasped Amber's hand and led her toward his camel, where he showed her which foot to put into the stirrup iron before getting her to swing her other leg over until she sat comfortably in the back of the saddle. Doing the same in front of her, he turned a little in the saddle and said to her, "When the camel begins to get up, lean way back in the saddle so that you don't tip forward.

Her surfing skills no doubt helped with her balance as she rocked back and then forward with the motion of the camel, while gripping the handhold in front. That Basam was directly in front of her also gave her greater confidence.

Though it was hot, the trek across the desert was no more than thirty minutes before the desert gave way to spindly trees and rocky ground. It greened up quickly once they navigated around trees and shrubs, with the loamy, earth scent becoming more prevalent and the increasing overhead shade cooling the searing air.

The sound of running water reached her ears minutes before they came to a big pool of water, where a waterfall cascaded into it from the far end of a rocky cliff edge and clumps of date palms reached high into the sky and threw out welcome shade.

She gaped. *This* wasn't what she'd expected! "Wow!"

Basam turned back to her and grinned. "I thought you might like it. If you know where to look, water can be found anywhere, even in the desert."

He turned his camel along a sandy path where there was plenty of shade from the trees, then got the camel to drop onto its haunches on command. The rest of the camels followed, allowing their riders to dismount.

Basam climbed off first, then reached out to help her off. She stumbled a little and he caught her, his eyes glinting as he looked down at her and said, "Careful, sunshine."

She smiled up at him, but pulled away at the malicious stare coming from behind. Maram. *Ugh.* That woman was a killjoy. She glanced down the line of camels and immediately found her. She looked wilted, sandy and infuriated.

Not the best combination.

Amber sent her a sunny smile, one that would no doubt piss her off a whole lot more, but she couldn't worry about the other woman's feelings. Amber was still too busy sorting out her own.

Basam soon enough directed everyone to help unload the pack camels, and though some of the guests grumbled under their breaths that it was a servant's job to do the menial work, many more looked happy to have half-a-day enjoying the outdoors with some of their closest friends.

Soon enough there were blankets on the ground with hampers set up in the middle. Cutlery, cups and plates came out next, along with bottles of water, wine and date arak. Fruit, salad, pita breads, cheeses and cold meats were unpacked last before everyone sat and filled their cups with their drink of choice.

Amber sat next to Basam, refusing to let it bother her when Maram took a seat on Basam's other side. If he was interested in the other woman he would have married her. He definitely wouldn't have gone to the trouble of setting up this fake girlfriend scenario.

So why did every husky laugh that came out of Maram's lush mouth make Amber's blood simmer? And why did Maram's every adoring, sideward gaze at Basam cause Amber's blood pressure to rise?

Everyone soon filled their plates with food and enjoyed the outdoor feast, their conversations becoming muted while the sun began to slowly fall toward the horizon.

"Would you care for another wine?" Basam asked.

Amber nodded. "Please."

He poured it into her tin cup. "My apologies that it's not in a fancy crystal glass, but I'm sure you can appreciate why."

"No apologies necessary," she said. "I like being a barbarian with you."

"I like it too," he admitted softly, lifting a hand then to brush some sand off her cheek. "You don't need a palace, fine clothes and jewels to be happy."

She smiled up at him. "Guess I'm a simple girl at heart."

Maram snorted, as though wholeheartedly agreeing. But suddenly Amber cared less about what the other woman thought, though she wasn't entirely sure if it was the wine or Basam's wholehearted attention that swayed her mindset.

Amber didn't need to play pretend when she sent him an adoring smile. Even knowing their partnership was fake, her heart sung every time he fed her a piece of succulent meat or fruit, his voice throaty as he murmured, "Try some of this." Or, "You've got to taste this."

Maram's good mood evaporated as she became withdrawn and angry. Amber bit her lip, guilt souring her joy at realizing the other woman really was in love with Basam, though whether it had anything to do with him being a sheikh was debatable.

Swallowing another mouthful of wine, she leaned forward to peer around Basam and ask Maram, "Do you mind if we chat...in private?"

Maram's gaze narrowed, then she nodded and said coolly, "Of course."

They stood and walked away from Basam and his guests who were still busy eating and intermittently conversing, but Amber was aware of Basam's eyes on her back as she and Maram headed around the pool of water toward the waterfall. Its spray brought welcome relief from the heat, while the noise of rushing water hopefully drowned out their conversation from the others.

Amber turned toward Maram. "I know you don't approve of Basam being with a western woman—"

"I don't approve of him being with *you*," she interjected bitterly, her dark eyes flashing. "It's easy to see you don't love him. You're just using him!"

"That's where you're wrong," Amber said softly. "I *do* love him. Unlike you though, I wish he wasn't a sheikh so that we had a real chance at being together."

"Except he *is* a sheikh and things will *never* work between you! You're a commoner. You were born as nothing and you will die as nothing!" Her hands curled into fists at her sides. "He'll realize soon enough you aren't the right woman for him. And if he doesn't, I'll make sure he does!"

Amber resisted rolling her eyes. She'd met dramatic people before, but this woman took the cake. "And how do you propose doing that?"

The other woman sneered, her face flushing with self-righteousness. "My father has a team of investigative journalists who I'm certain will uncover something about you. Everyone has secrets, right?" She was like a shark scenting blood as Amber gaped at her. "I have no doubt a scandal will be just the thing to break up your relationship with Basam. He won't have a choice but to walk away and end things with you."

Chapter Eleven

Though Basam lifted an enquiring eyebrow when Amber returned with Maram, there was nothing Amber wanted to say, she was still reeling by Maram's threat.

She sat next to him and gratefully accepted another drink, though it was water this time. At least now Amber understood why Basam didn't want anything to do with the other woman. She might be beautiful on the outside, but on the inside she was a nasty, mean person who wanted what she couldn't have.

The outing wasn't quite the same after the unpleasant face-to-face with Maram. Not even the delicious food and drinks, and the wonderful company—excluding one—could make up for Maram's intent to discredit Amber by uncovering her past.

Her stomach crunched. She no longer had any doubt that Maram's investigative journalists would unveil Amber's—her family's shameful history, then drag Basam's name through the mud along with her own. It wouldn't matter that she had a clean slate; her family didn't, so she'd be guilty by association.

"Give me ten minutes with Amber before you follow," Basam said to one of the men in the camel-riding party, interrupting her gloomy thoughts. He stood and reached for her hand, drawing her to her feet. "Come, there is something I want to show you."

She followed him hand-in-hand as he walked alongside the pool then turned and followed a rocky ledge that went behind the waterfall itself. The noise was powerful, ceaseless, and she laughed as she lifted her head to the fallout of spray that was wonderfully, gloriously cool.

Their companions were no longer visible through the wall of water, Basam taking advantage of that fact when the tugged her gently toward him. His head swooping low, his mouth claimed hers. His kiss was hot, insatiable, the spray of water now barely cooling her heated skin. It was only lucky his arm that was wrapped around her kept her stable, with her legs as shaky and unstable as her emotions.

Maram might have put a dampener on the outing, but the other woman was little more than a faded memory while she was in Basam's arms, his mouth tasting of decadence and pleasure.

It seemed forever yet no time at all before he drew back, his eyes burning and his thobe barely concealing the hard length of his arousal. "What are you doing to me, sunshine?" he asked hoarsely.

She licked her lips, and he groaned even as he took a step back and nodded behind her. "That wasn't the ten minutes I requested."

Of course it wasn't. She turned her head to see his guests approaching. It was no surprise to find Maram in the lead. The other woman didn't want Basam alone with Amber for any length of time. *Too little too late.* Though the falls cooled everything down, nothing could cool the passion burning inside her.

Basam might have experienced the same level of lust, but he was a gentleman by not showing it in front of his guests. Only Maram seemed aware of their heightened chemistry as she looked from one to the other and back again, her mouth tight and her movements stiff.

Basam allowed his guests ten minutes under the cooling spray before he hustled them all back to their camels, where he helped pack away the dishes, hampers and blankets before loading it onto the pack camels. Five minutes later they were all mounted, and their camels plodding steadily away from the lovely oasis.

"Thank you," she said quietly to his back, watching the way his body so easily swayed to his camel's loping walk.

He twisted in the saddle, looking back at her with warmth and some other, deeper emotion. "You're more than welcome, sunshine. I like nothing more than seeing you happy."

He turned back around to direct his camel, and though she was distracted again by his riding ability, she didn't need to guess whose scathing stare burned into her back. She exhaled slowly. She wouldn't let Maram spoil the experience yet again. She only had four more days left of the deal with Basam before she'd be returning home.

Never to see him again.

Her stomach wrenched but she managed to push away any further thoughts about her future. She was determined to just enjoy the remainder of the time she had here with him.

An eagle cried out overhead, and she tilted her head back to view the huge dark wings that were spread out high above her as the eagle drifted on warm air currents, its underside silhouetted by the sun that was closing in on the horizon.

There was such grandeur to the desert and sky out here, like the land and sky merged into one, then carried on forever, and she and everyone else on the planet were just temporary little blips in the cycle of life. It should have made her feel insignificant, instead she felt blessed to be here and to experience such a diverse way of life.

Servants hurried forward as Basam and his guests approached the palace on the camels. Basam commanded his camel to kneel and the other camels immediately followed suit. The riders dismounted, everyone appearing happy and content, while Maram marched away from the group and into the palace.

Amber winced. No doubt the horrid woman was on a mission to humiliate and smear her reputation as quickly as possible.

Basam glanced at Maram's retreating back, then looked back at Amber. "Anything you want to talk about?"

She shook her head. "Nothing you probably don't already know."

He was about to say something more when one of his guests approached and distracted him about some minor incident. Amber only wished Maram's threat was just as minor.

A few minutes later he left his servants to unload and attend to his prized camels, many of which she'd learned he'd bought from his good friend Sheikh Hamid. With his guests already disappearing inside the palace, he escorted Amber back to his suite of rooms and said, "I've arranged to have dinner in our rooms tonight."

She sagged gratefully. "Just you and me?"

He nodded. "No need for acting tonight, sunshine, though I have to say, I'm impressed. You've been amazing."

If only he knew how little effort she'd needed to put into the charade. She was about as defenseless against his charisma and good looks as the very woman he didn't want to marry.

She managed to pull together a smile. "Well I'm glad you didn't waste your money on me."

"On the contrary, I'd have paid double and still been happy."

It was next to impossible to ignore the swell of emotion inside her chest, or the absolute joy flooding through her. All she knew for sure was that she was balancing on the precipice of heartbreak, and it was time to take a giant step back.

*

If there was nothing better than having a long, hot shower and washing away the sand to feel clean again, then sitting in one of her modest nightgowns—created by the dressmaker, Marietta—while she stuffed her face with food had to be the next best thing.

No. Filling her stare with Basam in his simple gray T-shirt and soft white pants was the next best thing. No matter if her wore a thobe or a suit, or was dressed casually like now, he always looked superb. Even the growth on his jaw made her want to reach out and touch its roughness, then stroke

the smooth skin on the rest of his face.

She dragged her stare away from him to look down at her now half-empty plate. Their dinner had been nothing short of divine, with roast duck and potatoes, and steamed vegetables. The camel ride had increased her appetite, but she couldn't eat one more bite and she leaned back against her chair and said, "I'm so full I might explode!"

Basam smiled. "Care to sit out in the courtyard for a drink? The servants will clear this away tonight."

She nodded, touching the top of her head to ensure the messy bun she'd made do with was still holding together. "Thank you. That sounds lovely."

It *was* lovely. Though it was still balmy even with the night blanketing everything except for the gleam of the solar lights in the courtyard garden and the stars twinkling high overhead, there was something right to being outside. She lifted her face up to the heavens, absorbing the energy that all but thrummed around her.

"You really do love being outdoors, don't you," he mused.

She lifted her crystal glass and gulped down some of her wine. She only wished she could tell him she mostly just really loved being with him. But that was the last thing he'd want to hear. He'd have her bags packed and her money reversed back into his own account and all of this would have been for nothing.

She nodded. "I do." It wasn't a lie; it just wasn't the whole truth, either. She had her family to think about, her brother and her gorgeous niece. Not to mention her sister-in-law.

What about you?

She ignored the insidious voice inside her. She might have been selfless at the start, but she wasn't anywhere near selfless now. She wanted to get to know Basam more. She wanted to touch and kiss him again. She wanted to feel his body on top of hers and his cock stroking deep inside.

"Can I ask you one thing?" Basam murmured.

She stiffened, then nodded. "Of course."

"You asked for a hundred-thousand."

"Yes."

"Was it to repay your brother's gambling debts?"

She drained the last of her wine, needing its fortification, then she pushed back her chair and stood, too on edge now to be seated. "Does it matter?"

He pushed to his feet too, placing a hand on her shoulder then and gently turning her toward him. "It matters a lot."

She sighed, her head tilted back to look up at him. Damn, without heels she felt diminutive next to him. His height and the power he wielded always made her feel as though she was invincible when she was with him, like nothing could hurt her. She didn't feel that way now. She was cornered with nowhere to run. "If you must know, it *was* to repay his gambling debts," she conceded heavily.

"And if he gambles again, what then?" he asked softly.

"Then he's on his own." Literally. "And I can't help him anymore."

He gently plucked her empty glass from the death-grip of her hand, and put it onto the nearby table with his own. Then clasping either side of her head, he looked down at her and said, "Your selflessness only makes you more adorable, sunshine."

"You're pretty adorable yourself," she admitted in a croaky voice.

With deft fingers he pulled the pins out of her hair that restrained it, then watched it fall with wild, frizzy abandon around her face and down her back. "You really are my sunshine," he said reverently.

She might as well have been his stars and moon as well. No one had ever made her feel beautiful because of her hair. She'd mostly felt resigned to being born with such a frizzy mop that had a mind all of its own.

She shivered, all too aware she could easily love this man.

But none of that mattered right here, right now. All that mattered was getting closer to him. She was no longer scared to lose herself to him by being intimate; it was too late for that. She wanted to become his short-term lover and create memories she could hold onto for the rest of her life.

She pushed up onto her toes as he lowered his head, their mouths fusing together as one. Did he feel the crackle of electricity? He groaned against her lips. Perhaps he did. Then he swept his hands under her ass and lifted her against him. She wound her legs around his hips, her arms sliding around his nape as their kiss deepened.

She was only half-aware of him striding back inside of his suite of rooms, the automated lights switching on then back off again in their wake. He laid her onto his bed and followed her down. Only when he pulled his mouth away from hers did she ask huskily, "Is something wrong?"

He stroked back her hair, his eyes glowing. "I want to make sure this is what you want too. I don't want you having any regrets."

"Regrets?" She shook her head. "My only regret would be if we stopped now," she admitted softly.

Chapter Twelve

He groaned then, the sound curling her toes even before his mouth slammed back onto hers and he kissed her mercilessly hard. He pulled back just long enough to drag off her nightgown while she fumbled with his pants and T-shirt. Thankfully he'd gone commando underneath, his cock long and hard as she brushed her fingers against it.

His breath hissed, his whole body shuddering in ecstasy at her touch. She inhaled sharply. If he was so sensitive to her brushing against him, what would he do if she clasped his shaft and dragged her hand up and down?

He reached between her thighs, zeroing in on her clit and deftly massaging. All thought ceased and she gasped as pleasure accosted her, burning through her nerve endings and heightening her pleasure a hundred fold. She writhed against him, then finally pulled her head back, his form above a blur as her senses honed in on his touch. "I-I can't take much more," she whimpered.

"Oh, but you will," he countered silkily, his eyes flaming with volcanic intensity. "I want you to feel the explosion and see the fireworks. I want you to burn for me, sunshine."

She was almost there already, her body sizzling and aroused to the point of no return—when he took away his hand and left her poised at the very edge. Her breath hissed out. "Wh-what are you doing?"

He reached into the drawer of his side table and extracted a foil. "Protection," he said hoarsely, taking off its wrapper then and pulling on a condom with economical swiftness.

Her womb fluttered along with her pulse. Once again he was taking care of everything. She'd been so lost to passion she hadn't even considered any future consequences.

He touched between her thighs again, this time with a gentle caress that climbed her straight back up to where she'd been left hanging. "So passionate," he said with a smile that appeared to be as tortured as her body was for release.

He pushed a finger inside her and she moaned at the intimacy of it. When he pushed a second finger inside her, then withdrew most of the way out before plunging back inside again, she automatically counterthrusted against him.

"And so damn wet," he growled. "You'll need to be to take all of me inside."

She stiffened, but he'd already guided his cock to her entrance, his eyes burning into hers. She waited, fear and adrenaline making her pulse surge. Then he slammed his cock inside her and her breath rushed out, his size brutal despite her body's welcoming lubrication.

He paused, waiting for her inner muscles to adjust. "Tell me you're okay?"

She fought back a grimace as she nodded, then gyrated against him. "Never. Better."

He didn't recognize her lie, of course he didn't. His mind would be too busy fighting with his body, the strain of not rocking inside her showing in his every taut line, his every locked muscle. He nodded even as he withdrew from her partway, then surged back inside her.

She swallowed hard, caught between pleasure and pain, and he repeated the movement, driving into her harder and faster until he was nothing short of a pounding machine. Picking up one of her legs, he pushed it back, changing the angle of penetration.

It was enough for her to reach the peak, then abandon all sense of reality as she blasted high into the heavens, fireworks exploding all around her as she floated in orgasmic bliss, before freefalling back to Earth.

Basam cradled her with one arm as he stroked once, twice, then jerked hard inside her as he roared with what had to be a supernova release, his eyes rolling and his jaw clenching, his skin damp against her.

They were both breathing heavily when he collapsed over her, then rolled to his side, bringing her with him. They stayed that way for long, intangible minutes, then kissing her on the forehead, he withdrew from her and climbed out of bed to dispose of the condom.

She was fighting to stay awake when he returned as nude as he'd departed, completely unselfconscious. Little wonder. Not only did he have the muscled body of a demigod, his cock was large even when it was deflated from sex.

She'd never been so sated in her life, the aftereffect of sex better than any drug or sweet lullaby to make her fall to sleep. But then being joined with him had transcended anything she'd experienced in the past. Sex with other men had been lackluster at best.

"Do you know how beautiful you look right now?" he asked huskily, his eyes drinking her in. "You have an after-sex glow that makes me want to claim you all over again." As if proving his theory, his cock jerked and thickened, ready for another round.

He joined her on top of the covers, the bedroom light still glowing above as he turned to her and touched the left side of his chest, stating softly, "You're getting to me right in here."

It wasn't a declaration of love, but it was more than enough for her. It'd only been four days since she'd spilled wine all over him and already their feelings were growing deep. How much deeper would they get once her seven day contract was completed?

He drew her close and kissed her, and this time it was slow, tender and gentle. He pulled back. "As much as I'd love a repeat performance, you need your sleep," he said huskily. His lazy smile belied the passion behind his eyes. "You'll be glad to know you can sleep in tomorrow morning though."

"Oh?"

"I've got meetings planned for most of the day, ones I can't get out of. My people don't appreciate it when my grand vizier takes my place to dish out advice."

"Do you ever stop being a sheikh?" she asked drowsily.

"Not often. Despite what many people believe, I serve my country and its people, not the other way around."

Her lashes trembled, then swept closed, his words echoing in her ears even as darkness finally claimed her.

*

She was running downstairs, her tiny feet slapping against the wooden steps. Thanks to the laughter and noise from the lounge room, she hadn't been able to get to sleep. But she was nine years old now, big enough to ask everyone to please be quiet.

She was halfway through the aged kitchen when she wrinkled her nose, her nostrils stinging. She'd been noticing the distinct smell on and off for weeks now. It was disgusting, like burned plastic or rubber.

She pushed open the door to a cloud of smoke billowing into her face. She choked and coughed, her eyes watering as she blinked and forced back a sudden desire to run far away. Instead she focused inside the room.

Her dad was sucking on some kind of pipe, inhaling deeply before he passed it to his friend. She turned to her mother. She was wild-eyed and frazzled, her tone sharp when she spoke. "Amber, what are you doing down here? It's your bedtime!"

Amber gaped. Her mom's eyes didn't look right, her dad glaring balefully at her now with cold, red eyes.

"What are you staring at girl?" her dad slurred, picking up a glass bottle with reddish-brown liquid in and taking a mouthful from it. "I served my country. I have every right now to live my life how I want to. Now get back up to bed before my good mood disappears."

"Go on then," her mom added. "Scoot!"

Amber didn't stick around to argue. Her eyes were stinging from the horrid smoke, or was it from the tears knowing she and Zach would be taking care of themselves again for the next few days? There'd be no packed lunches, no ironed uniforms, just angry and hateful parents.

She pushed shut the door and turned away. As she stomped up the stairs she knew one thing was sure. When she grew up she was never going to be like her mom or dad.

Chapter Thirteen

She woke the next day aware Basam was long gone. That he'd woken her earlier in the morning to his drugging kisses that had soon turned to licking and sucking at her most intimate place was something that, even now, thrilled her to the marrow of her bones.

She'd climaxed hard and fast under his mouth, then he'd kissed her with the taste of her orgasm on his mouth before he'd turned her onto her stomach and taken her from behind, pumping into her like a machine on steroids.

He'd been insatiable.

He'd made her nightmare fade as if it'd never been from the moment he'd kissed her awake. But now she was left wondering if maybe she *had* inherited her parents' unhealthy addiction. If her mom and dad had been addicted to drugs and booze, and her brother was addicted to gambling, then she just might be addicted to Basam.

She grinned sleepily. There were worse habits to have. Maybe tonight it'd be her turn to pleasure him. She'd take him into her mouth and make him fall apart just like he'd made her fall apart.

Knock. Knock. Knock.

She climbed out of bed and grabbed an abaya out of her closet and dragged it on. A pity there was no time to pin back her bedroom hair or at least make it half-presentable. She probably looked exactly how she felt—like she'd been thoroughly fucked half the night.

She padded to the front door and swung it open to a young boy who looked a little fearfully at the guards standing guard either side of her door. "Hello there," she said with a smile. "What can I do for you?"

"Are you Amber?" he asked in a high voice. At her nod, he handed her an envelope. "Then this is for you."

"Thank you," she said, accepting it with a strange feeling of foreboding.

She went to close the door when he added, "I'm to stay with you until you read the note inside."

She arched a brow. "Okay, then. Come in."

One of the guards looked her way with a frown. "We're under strict instructions not to let anyone past these doors."

She almost giggled. Basam was getting rather protective. "I think I'm safe enough. He's all of eight years old."

"Ten," the boy corrected in an aggrieved voice.

The guard reluctantly nodded. "Very well." He glanced at the boy. "Make it quick."

The boy stepped inside, then waited as she shut door behind them and opened the letter. She pulled out a document and began reading bullet points showcasing every dark and dirty secret her family had, with some she hadn't even been aware of.

Her hands shook as she pushed the evidence back into its envelope, trepidation and foreboding filling her even before she looked back at the boy. "Who sent you?"

He shrugged his thin shoulders. "Maram did. She said if you know what's good for you, you'll follow me to where she's waiting in her suite of rooms."

Amber was numb then, her emotions compartmentalized so that she didn't fall apart. "Wait here then while I tidy myself up."

Tidying her hair back into its usual bun, with Basam's gift of jewels around her throat and in her ears, she slipped on some heeled shoes and walked back to where the boy patiently waited. "I guess I'm ready," she said.

She followed him out of her suite of rooms and down a maze of corridors. "You seem to know your way around here very well."

He nodded. "My mom works here in the kitchens. The palace is my playground."

It made sense. Maram had probably bribed him to get him to give her the note. She clearly didn't mind using children to get what—*who*—she wanted.

"This wing is where the guests stay," the young boy informed her, before he turned right into yet another corridor, then knocked on the third door to the left.

As it swung open, Maram looked from Amber to the boy, then handed him another envelope, this one no doubt filled with money. "Well done, Aaben."

He hurried off, clutching the envelope to his chest, then disappeared back to wherever in the palace he'd come from.

Maram smiled gloatingly at Amber, her eyes glinting. That she'd dressed for the confrontation was obvious. From her emerald green abaya that was drawn in tight at her waist to her dark hair that tumbled down her back, her kohl eyes and red lips, she'd clearly primped and preened for hours. "I'm so glad you knew better than to ignore my message," she said huskily

Amber kept her face empty and her voice neutral. I'm doing what has to be done, nothing more."

Maram looked both ways down the corridor. Satisfied no one was around, she gestured for Amber to come inside.

She glanced at the suite of rooms, the gold and pearl-blue tones of the furnishings a beautiful match to the white walls with gold trim. The only thing off-putting was the floral scent Maram must have sprayed liberally all over her body. It was sickeningly sweet.

"Please, take a seat," Maram said regally, like she imagined she was already the sheikha of the palace.

Amber headed to the comfortable sofas and armchairs that faced one another, the handcrafted coffee table sitting between them already showcasing a tray with an intricately patterned, silver teapot called a samovar. There were also biscuits on a little plate, along with nuts and dried fruits.

She selected an armchair as Maram took the one opposite.

"Would you like some mint tea?" Maram asked.

"Thank you, but no thank you." She wouldn't put it past the other woman to have poisoned it.

"Suit yourself." She sniggered, leaning forward then to pour herself a cup of the steaming tea, its mint aroma filling the air. She took a long sip, then inhaled happily and said, "It seems addiction runs in your family. Tell me...what is yours?"

Basam. He was all she wanted, all she'd ever want.

"Not that it matters," Maram said with a shark-like smile. "I have enough newsworthy facts here to sink the Titanic all over again...dragging you down with it."

"You'd love that, wouldn't you?"

She clucked her tongue. "Now, now. There's no reason to get nasty."

Was this woman serious? She was the queen of nastiness!

Maram reached for a biscuit, then crunched down on it with her sharp teeth. "I guess you want to know how to stop the information I've acquired about your family? I mean, you wouldn't want any of it getting out to the public, would you?"

"And I'm guessing you already have a suitable bribe to stop that happening?"

"Oh my, how did you get to be so cynical?" she asked, another laugh peeling apart her red, shining lips. She took another delicate sip of her tea, her eyes appraising Amber. "I did warn you that everyone has a past, didn't I?"

"Yet mine is flawless."

Maram sighed dramatically. "Unfortunately, the same can't be said about your family. Not only did your dear mother and father get charged with neglect numerous times, they drove while intoxicated and heavily under the influence of drugs. The car accident that killed them also killed an innocent motorist. A young lady with her whole life ahead of her."

After all the years of guilt that had weighed heavily on her through no fault of her own, Amber struggled to breathe evenly while keeping her heart from bouncing out of her chest. It was bad enough never fully grieving for her parents who were never really parents in any sense of the word other than biological.

Knowing someone innocent had been killed because of them, a woman who'd left behind her own family to grieve for her and be enraged by the injustice of it all was enough to make Amber want to rip out her own hair and howl her grievances. Instead she suppressed her emotions, locked them back away in their box where they couldn't hurt her.

"I see I've hit a sore spot." Maram spoke with absolute indifference while Amber's world threatened to collapse around her. "No doubt your brother's gambling debts have also plagued you badly. But I'm willing to offer you a chance to make this all go away—by having *you* go away—and as a gesture of goodwill, I'll even throw in the hundred-thousand needed to make your life less...stressful."

"Basam will never believe I left of my own free will." Yet her words were as empty as her spirit. She'd fought for so long she no longer had any fight left to give.

Maram cocked her head to the side. "Not even if you write him a letter and leave it on your bed?"

"And tell him what? That I had a change of heart?"

He'd never believe it, would he?

"Yes, that's it exactly. Tell him you miss your beaches, your surf and sun. Tell him you miss your meat pies and sausages on the barbecue. Tell him whatever you know he'll believe and he'll never have to face the scandal and shame of your family's infamy."

Amber wilted against her armchair. Basam's people would never understand her side of the story. She'd be nothing short of a piranha thanks to her parents' irresponsible lifestyle and utter neglect. She'd be painted the villain and Basam would be crucified for even having her under the same roof as him.

Even if Amber *did* matter to him as much as she hoped, Maram would be here to ease his loneliness and ensure he'd soon forget about the clumsy, common Australian waitress he'd brought to his country for a short time.

A surge of guilt threatened to break through the box inside and crush her. If she left now Basam might never fully trust a woman again, her deal with him broken, her promise to him voided. But if she stayed she'd hurt him a whole lot more. His reputation would be in tatters.

"Well?" the other woman prompted. "What's your answer?"

She looked at the other woman without really seeing her. "How soon can you get me home?"

Chapter Fourteen

Amber dropped her pen and folded her letter, her vision blurry and her emotions stark. She didn't want to leave Basam, not like this. But what choice did she have? He'd hate her if she left. He'd hate her even more if she stayed and he had to deal with a scandal that would rock his status as sheikh.

She sniffled, placing her letter onto her pillow where he'd see it before she placed the jewelry beside it. If her words didn't turn him away, seeing her abandon her gifts just like she was abandoning him should do the trick.

As much as a part of her longed for him to chase after her and beg for her to return, she knew it was an impossible dream. Being with him again meant having her family's dark past exposed and creating a mess that not even Basam could clean up. It was a no-win situation all round.

She sighed heavily, looking around the bedroom one last time to imprint it on her brain. Then grabbing her suitcase, she wheeled it behind her and stepped through the lounge room and dining room, then finally through the sitting room where she pushed open the double doors and stepped through.

The two men standing guard looked at one another before one of them asked, "Basam knows you're leaving?"

She lifted her chin. "He will soon enough." She managed a smile that trembled at the corners of her lips. "Take care of him for me, won't you?"

The guard nodded uneasily, the other one shuffling his feet. They clearly didn't want her to go, but they'd also clearly been told not to interfere. She was, after all, here of her own free will.

And that was how she'd leave.

"Goodbye," she said, her voice cracking. She would not cry. Not here. Not in front of Basam's men.

Lifting her chin and blinking back tears, she stalked away from them and down one corridor after another toward Maram's suite of rooms. When Amber finally arrived, Maram was already at her opened door, gesturing for her to hurry.

Maram pulled her inside and shut and locked the door. She looked at her with sharp, assessing eyes. "You wrote the letter?"

Amber nodded. "I did."

Maram's smile was almost reflected in her dark stare. "It would seem you're not such a simple girl at heart, after all?" She giggled, then said in a warmer tone, "Come, I know a back way we can go."

She led her outside to a courtyard, the sun insidiously hot even under the date palms rustling branches. Opening a door at the other end of the outdoor area, Maram hustled her inside yet another corridor.

Though this side of the palace would still be considered grand, it wasn't nearly as glamorous as the wings of the palace Amber had been shown.

"This is the servants' wing," Maram said in an undertone. "Hopefully they'll all be too busy to go running off informing Basam of your departure."

Amber followed her through a few more corridors, the palace once again looking extravagant and elegant, with mosaic floors and high arched ceilings. The walls of this corridor showcased the sunrise and sunsets of desert landscapes and, despite her despair, a distant part of her couldn't help but admire each of them as she walked past.

Then they passed an opened doorway of a huge room featuring black and white floor tiles. She didn't have a chance to look inside, but she noticed the workmen who were busy rebuilding and transforming the area.

She glanced at Maram. "What is that room?"

Maram sent her a quick look, her eyes speculative. "A ballroom apparently. He recently commissioned an architect and builder to begin work on it." Her lip curled and her voice cooled. "It's becoming quite a tradition for sheikhs to have one."

A little shiver skated down Amber's spine. The ballroom would be beautiful once it was done. It'd take what? A month? Six months, before it was finished? Though she was certain Basam would pay well to have the ballroom finished as fast as possible.

"I can't wait to see it when it's done," Maram added vindictively. She liked rubbing in the fact Amber would never have that same privilege.

"I'm sure it will be beautiful," she said tonelessly.

"It will be even more beautiful when I'm dancing across the checkered floor in Basam's arms."

Amber almost snorted. The woman was delusional. Basam would never want Maram in that way. She suspected even being friends was becoming doubtful in his eyes.

Soon enough they exited the side of the palace where more date palms stood sentry, a dozen or more of them surrounding a white-pebbled driveway that gleamed under the sun. A large black sedan waited close by, its chauffeur looking hot and bothered as he stood beside an opened back door.

"Well, this is where I leave you," Maram said with a cool smile. "You'll have your money in your bank account tonight."

"Wait. I haven't given you my bank account details."

"Do you really think I need them?" she scoffed. "I've got more on you than you probably do yourself." Her red lips curled into a smile that bordered on a sneer. "Goodbye Amber, please don't make me regret being nice to you."

This was her being nice?

She wasted all of ten seconds watching Maram strut back the way she'd come, all long flowing black hair and swishing green abaya. Then Amber took one last, long look at the beautiful palace before she turned and stepped toward her getaway car.

Chapter Fifteen

Basam stalked down the corridor of his palace with his thoughts no longer on his people's problems or that of his country. He had an uncanny ability to solve everything that came his way, no matter how complicated, so he wasn't concerned about the empty threats or pressures placed on his shoulders.

His every thought now centered on the woman he'd made love to last night, a woman he couldn't get out of his head even in the thick of a deep grievance between neighbors he'd eventually resolved.

Many believed love made a man weak. He believed love made a man strong, invincible. Powerful. In that moment he had enough conviction inside him to take on the world.

His lips pulled into a wide smile as he turned and headed toward his suite of rooms. He had so much to talk to Amber about, not least of all requesting that she stay for the foreseeable future. His contract would soon run out, and he couldn't bear the thought of losing her.

He already had ideas to build a huge wave pool and beach. She could teach the no doubt many interested surfers-to-be or just simply enjoy the wave pool to herself, he didn't mind, as long as she was happy.

Tomorrow he intended to show her falconry, he was certain she'd enjoy that, then he'd take her to the markets where she could shop till she dropped. They needed a day together. Maram's father had already accepted Basam wasn't interested in his daughter—he'd even admitted gruffly that Amber seemed like a wonderful, caring woman.

Once the ballroom was completed—it couldn't happen soon enough!—he'd show her it before he proposed to her. Nothing could possibly change his mind about how he felt about her. He'd been in denial too long already. She'd captured his attention and now she'd captured his heart.

He was certain his people would love her as much as he did. She was caring and beautiful, as bright as a star and twice as radiant.

He slowed a little at seeing the guards at the front doorway to his suite of rooms, their nervousness all too apparent. He stopped in front of them, his pulse suddenly drumming in his ears. "Is everything all right?"

"Sheikh Basam," one of them said, bowing his head. "Your guest, Amber Clayton, is no longer here."

He frowned even as his heart bottomed out and left him reeling. "She's...gone?"

"I believe so," the same guard conceded. He cleared his throat. "A young boy came to see her. She followed him somewhere, then returned alone to her rooms before she dragged out one piece of luggage behind her." He glanced at the other guard, then added, "She seemed...upset, and asked us to take care of you."

"And you allowed her to go?" he growled.

"We had no choice, Sheikh Basam, not after you ordered us to leave her to come and go as she pleased." The guard swallowed convulsively. "We didn't dare try to stop her."

Fuck. He couldn't blame his men, they'd done as he'd asked. "I want you both to go and get me Abdul." He was head of security. "Tell him I want every piece of footage showing Amber and anyone who was with her from today."

They nodded and all but ran to do as he requested. He pushed open his door and stepped inside, aware immediately she'd gone. Her lack of presence in the suite of rooms was like a void, an empty vacuum. He stalked through the rooms, checking each one for any clues or information. Only once he stalked into the bedroom did he notice the jewelry he'd gifted her was left on the pillow of his bed, along with a letter.

He swore under his breath, his heart surging even as he stepped forward and grabbed the letter. Opening it with unsteady hands, he scanned her handwriting and read what couldn't possibly be true.

He reread it again just to be sure.

Dear Basam,

I know even as I write this that I'm going to hurt you one way or the other, but believe me that isn't and has never been my intention. I can't tell you enough how much I enjoyed every minute I spent with you. Last night was incredible. But my heart doesn't belong here, it belongs back home at the beaches I love and the children I teach. It belongs with the foamy waves that hit the sandy shore and the sun that shines bright on the ocean.

But most of all, it belongs with my brother and my niece. They're my only family now and I can't lose them, not even for you.

I know I've broken my contract and I fully expect and want you to take back the money you offered. I know you'll find the woman of your dreams, whoever she may be, just as I know she'll make you happier than I ever could. Your people will love her too, I'm sure.

I'm just honored to have known you for this brief but wonderful time.

All I ask is that you please don't hate me.

Amber xxx

His heart contracted even as his vision misted with red and his hands fisted, crumpling the letter before he straightened the page and read it all over again. He was no masochist, but something didn't add up. What had she meant by *hurt you one way or the other*? And why would she want him to take back the money when it was the one and only way to save her brother?

Nothing made sense and nothing added up.

Luckily he was a master at fixing problems and he intended to solve this one sooner rather than later, because he couldn't lose his sunshine. He couldn't lose the love of his life.

Chapter Sixteen

Amber looked through her binoculars as seawater touched her toes before it was sucked back out into the deeper ocean, where five of her students were doing amazingly well catching waves.

That they were teenagers didn't mean she'd take her eyes off them. The ocean could be unpredictable and unforgiving even when every rule was followed to a T.

She adjusted her straw hat and flexed her toes in the sand as another wave surged toward her in full force, breaking apart seconds later and becoming a long stream of approaching water that was still incredibly powerful.

Three of her students caught the next wave in, their ability to ride their surfboards amazing to watch. They'd all come so far in a short time and she couldn't be more proud of them.

She high-fived each one of them as they came out of the surf before they headed to the surf school building to wash off the boards and place them on their wall racks. It wasn't until the last two came in and she watched them trudge across the sand and into the building that she tossed her straw hat and binoculars onto her towel, then picked up her surfboard jammed into the sand beside her.

The other surf school staff would ensure the teenagers were delivered safely to their parents, which meant she was free now to enjoy the waves herself.

She ran into the ocean and jumped onto her surfboard on her belly, duck-diving under the first breaking wave, then pushing back up to the surface to continue paddling out just behind the white water of the break zone. Her whole body hummed, joy lighting her from the inside out.

If she couldn't have Basam, then this was the next best thing. It'd been six weeks since she'd last seen him and today was the first real glimmer of delight she'd had since she'd left.

Though a part of her had hoped he'd chase after her, she knew it was for the best that he hadn't. They were from two completely different worlds. They had never been meant to be. She only hoped Maram hadn't managed to sink her claws into him, he deserved far better than that woman.

That Basam's hundred-thousand was still in her account—it'd been Maram's blackmail money that had paid off Zach's debts—made her feel worse instead of better. She didn't need his money sitting there day and night, not when it reminded her of the man she was trying so desperately to forget. That a part of her was glad she still had backup money in case her brother relapsed again infuriated her.

She didn't want contradictory, seesawing emotions to consume her. She wanted to live her life without tension and stress. She wanted to teach people to surf while continuing to have the luxury to surf herself. That she also still wanted Basam was yet another contradictory need that pulled at her in opposite directions.

That one could never come with the other was insufferable. It was Basam or it was her family along with beaches and surfing.

She paddled to the lineup where nearly a dozen other surfers waited for the next big wave. A young blond dude looked at her with eyes full of sympathy and asked, "Are you okay?"

Oh shit. She'd been crying and hadn't even been aware of it.

She managed a smile and said, "The seawater is killing my eyes, but I'm addicted. Nothing can keep me away from the ocean."

Her brother wasn't alone with his addiction. Hers were beginning to add up.

The young blond dude grinned. "Know what you mean. I got wiped out on the last wave and now I'm back for another round."

A wave started to build and four of the waiting surfers paddled fast to catch it. Amber was just glad to lie on her board and let the water carry all her thoughts and worries away.

Who needed a therapist or pills when Mother Nature was on hand to provide all the calming influence she needed? One day she might even stop thinking about Basam and get back into the dating scene.

Seeing Zach and Rachel become so gloriously happy again together, and their daughter, Katie, blossoming under their nurturing love and care, made her think perhaps it was possible to find someone a second time.

That's never going to happen. Love at first sight is so unlikely it borders on mythical. You know no one will make you feel anything close to how you did with Basam.

She squeezed her eyes closed, her chest aching as much as her fingers did that gripped the edges of her board. Even if she never connected with someone immediately like she had with Basam, perhaps she'd settle for friendship first and allow it to build into something romantic.

More surfers took off with the next big wave, leaving her and the blond surfer alone to catch the next one. She waited, nodding at the blond dude as an incoming wave built. She paddled furiously beside him, then stood effortlessly balanced on her board.

There was no greater feeling, besides sex, than the adrenaline of catching an awesome wave, then carving along the top of it before pivoting sharply to ride down its face.

She was beaming, lost in the moment as she finished her ride, jumping off her board then wading through the undercurrent as she carried her board to shore. Some of her frizzy hair had escaped her scraped-back ponytail, and she pushed some strands behind her ear before she jammed her board into some loose dry sand, then peeled off her wetsuit to her bikini beneath.

Once her surf lessons had finished for the day, it'd become routine for her to sit on the beach for ten minutes while the sun kissed her skin and dried her off, the crashing waves a beautiful symphony she'd never get tired of hearing

She closed her eyes, enjoying the serenity when a tread sounded from behind.

"I thought I might find you here, sunshine."

Chapter Seventeen

Amber gaped, her heart pounding so hard she had to be close to passing out. Basam stood behind her in dark chinos and a white T-shirt, and looking so impossibly handsome she almost wept.

"Nothing to say?" he asked.

She shook her head. "Why are you here? Y-you can't be here!"

"Is that right?" he asked, his brilliant golden eyes narrowing.

Shit. She couldn't tell him the truth, and yet already she was giving herself away. She nodded. "I've already said what I had to say."

"You didn't *say* anything," he reminded succinctly. "You left me a note."

"I-I did," she acknowledged.

"Why?" he growled. "What made you leave?'"

"I explained—"

"You explained nothing!" he interjected

She swallowed hard. "Please don't do this."

"Do what? Demand the truth?"

"It's taken you six weeks to decide you want more from me than the note?"

"It's taken me that long to organize everything that I wanted done before I brought you back."

"Back?" she asked weakly, her senses reeling as hope built inside, then shattered all over again when she realized it was an impossibility. Maram would release the information she'd so far withheld about Amber's family, information that would cripple Basam's leadership. "I-I can't go back."

His jaw tightened along with his shoulders. "Tell me you'd happily watch me turn away and walk out of your life forever. If so I'll leave right now and you'll never see me again."

"That's blackmail," she gritted.

"And yet that was why you ran away in the first place, was it not?"

He knew.

She blinked, her stomach pitching. "What do you mean?"

"You know exactly what I'm talking about, Amber."

Her mouth dropped open. He'd rarely used her real name. *Whatever.* She couldn't sit on the sand for a second longer, not while he towered over her like some avenging angel. She pushed to her feet and still felt insignificant. She tilted up her chin and said, "What do you want me to say?"

"The truth would be good."

He wanted the truth...then he'd get it!

"The truth is you deserve someone better, someone without a history who could ruin your relationship with your people. The truth is I can't leave my family or the ocean. My life is here! I can't give it up."

There, she'd said it. He didn't need to know she'd give up absolutely everything for him, just as long as she was able to visit her family regularly.

"Not for anyone," she added, lying right through her teeth.

Desperate times called for desperate measures.

He cocked his head to the side. "What if you found out your brother has secretly been gambling again?"

She swayed, the man in front of her becoming as indistinct as the sound of the waves and a seagull squawking somewhere in the distance. "You're lying."

"I'm not lying," he said quietly. "I haven't ever lied to you."

She lowered her lashes to hide her eyes as she pushed back tears. "What do you want from me?"

"Come home with me, complete the four days of your contract and I'll make sure Zach gets the help he needs. Counseling. Hypnosis. Alternative medicine. Even drug therapy, if it's needed." His eyes glinted. "And you get to keep that extra hundred-thousand in your bank."

She looked back up. "Why?" she asked, her voice cracking. "I thought you'd hate me now."

He shook his head. "I could never hate you, sunshine." He grimaced. "I've reserved that for the woman who conspired against us and left you with little choice but to leave."

So he really *did* know everything then. Her shoulders sagged and she studied the sand. How many billions of grains must there be just where they stood? More importantly, how had this charismatic sheikh returned for her when everyday men hadn't bothered to stick around long enough to care about her inner beauty? Her eyes burned as she looked back up at him. "I'm sorry."

"I don't want your apology," he stated roughly, reaching out to cup her chin with one hand and lifting her gaze to meet his. "I want you."

She managed a watery smile. "Then how can I say no."

His amber gaze warming, he bent, his lips that brushed across hers firing up her nerve endings and reminding her just how much she *did* want him. He pulled back, his gaze stark. "Our jet is waiting."

A little over an hour later she was climbing the steps to his jet, feeling a little self-conscious that she was wearing nothing more than her sandals and the sundress she'd thrown over her bikini before she'd left her house. Her wetsuit, towel and straw hat had been left in her locker inside the surf school building.

She took one of the luxurious leather seats right next to the window, wincing as she imagined the sand and salt she'd leave behind. Basam sat next to her as the jet's engine started, and the same pretty brunette air hostess approached them once again, her eyes widening at seeing Amber and no doubt questioning Basam's taste.

The brunette no doubt remembered the passionate kiss Amber and Basam had shared at the jet's open door while the press had snapped images of them both. It had been day two of her contract. It could have been yesterday even as it could have been a hundred years ago.

"Sheikh Basam," the air hostess said reverently. She smiled and nodded at Amber. "Amber, it's lovely to see you again."

She resisted touching her corkscrew hair that was barely restrained now. "You too," she managed.

The air hostess beamed. "Would you like something to drink before takeoff?"

Basam looked at Amber. "Champagne?"

She nodded. "That would be wonderful."

She hadn't touched a drop since returning to Australia, but suddenly she needed alcoholic reinforcement. Anything to dull her heightened emotions, including the flood of guilt for what she'd done to Basam.

They had just enough time to drink their fruity bubbly before the air hostess retrieved their glasses, the jet slowly taxiing toward the runway.

Only once they'd taken off and reached altitude did Basam unclip her seatbelt, then his, and said, "I think a shower is in order."

She nodded. She'd never been so keen to wash the salt water out of her hair and the sand off her body. And she had no doubt he'd brought along half the wardrobe of clothes she'd left behind. "I'd love that."

The glint in his eyes told her that he had no objection, either.

A surge of thrilling anticipation started low in her stomach before flooding through her body. She needed Basam's mouth on hers and his body inside her. One night with him hadn't been anywhere near enough, she was greedy for him.

He took her hand as they walked down the aisle, then turned into the bedroom. He shut the door behind them, his mouth claiming hers once again as they began pulling off each other's clothes.

They didn't make it to the bathroom. They were both naked when he tipped her onto the bed and climbed on top of her, his mouth again pressing onto hers as he reached down and rubbed her clit with an expertise that left her gasping beneath him, her body quaking.

He was poised over her, his cock aligned to her center, when he drove inside her. She gasped. *Holy shit!* He was bare inside her and it felt wonderful. But she wasn't ready for an accidental pregnancy.

She tore her mouth from his. "We're not protected."

His amber eyes gleamed. "I'm clean and I know you are."

Of course he did. He'd probably researched her more thoroughly now than Maram had. She squirmed a little beneath him even as she managed a glare. "I don't want to get pregnant."

His smile looked pained. "I'll pull out."

She was too far gone to argue there was still a chance his pre-cum could get her pregnant. She was just glad the odds were far less likely. Then he began to stroke inside her and she would have been lucky to remember her name. Everything was centered on the pleasure building inside her.

He kneeled, lifting her flush against him, then stroked deeper and harder, the different angle hitting a place inside her that pushed her straight into orgasm, her strangled shout as she climaxed violently probably heard by everyone onboard. In that moment she didn't care, she surrendered completely to Basam, her whole body shuddering as her inner muscles clenched and released.

He slid out, then erupted with a hoarse groan, his seed pulsating over her breasts, marking her. He reinforced it with a growled, "You're mine, sunshine."

Chapter Eighteen

Amber climbed out of the car and was immediately hit with a heatwave thanks to the midday sun.

She smiled. It was just like coming home again.

The feeling only grew as she followed Basam into his palace, where two of his guards bowed their heads. He nodded back to them before he continued through the palace, but instead of taking her to his suite of rooms, he directed her along some other corridors.

"Where are we going?"

"If I told you, it wouldn't be a surprise."

It was only when they traversed through the corridor where pictures of desert landscapes were hung that she realized where they were most likely heading. She glanced at him. "You're taking me to the ballroom."

His brow furrowed as he looked at her. "How did you—"

He shook his head. "Of course, Maram took you this way so that fewer people noticed you leave."

She nodded. "How did you know?"

"Security footage. Of course, she still denied it even when I confronted her about it."

Of course Maram would act innocent while proclaiming everyone else's guilt. Amber slowed, then stopped and asked, "Did she tell you she found skeletons in my closet, ones that might very well turn your people against you?"

He pivoted to face her, "Yes, she did. What she didn't seem to care about was the fact those skeletons weren't yours, they were your parents." His eyes held hers. "I honestly believe the majority of my people will love you regardless of what secrets might be exposed by Maram or anyone else."

Amber swallowed hard. "Would they love me knowing my parents were drink and drug driving when they hit another car and killed an innocent woman inside it?"

He lifted his hands to her shoulders. "Stop carrying the burden of other people's wrongs. You were an innocent child, they were irresponsible adults. The blame lies with them, not with you."

Though a part of her had acknowledged she'd played no part in the woman's or her parents' death, she hadn't been able to shake off the insidious guilt. So why did Basam's words of reassurance become a revelation etched deep into her soul, an epiphany wiping away her guilt and tearing the weight off her shoulders?

"Thank you," she said softly.

"For telling you the truth?" he asked gently. "You're an amazing woman, sunshine, and despite your internal scars thanks to your parents' lack of care, you're beautiful inside *and* out. I couldn't love you more."

Her heart pounded and her chest tingled, her eyes locking onto his. "You really mean that, don't you?"

His smile was warm, his stare adoring. He reached for her hand, his thumb rubbing her palm in a circular motion and weakening the last of her resolve. "Let me prove it to you," he said huskily.

She followed him just a few more steps before turning into the now completed ballroom. She gasped, her gaze roaming around the cavernous and magnificent room, from the black-and-white checkered floor to the high ceiling with a trio of glittering chandeliers. There was some tiered platforms on her right, which she guessed was for a small orchestra or musicians, and seating and a long bar to her left.

"What's this all about?"

"I had it built for you."

"For me?" she squeaked, her mind racing with questions that had no answers. "Why?"

He smiled. "I guess you haven't heard of the recent trend—thanks to a wager that was started between some good sheikh friends of mine—where each of them had to build a ballroom the moment they lost their hearts to a woman."

She blinked at him. "Maram mentioned something about it being a tradition for sheikhs to have one. But you must have starting building this—"

"The day I brought you back to my country."

She felt the blood drain out of her face. "I-I don't know what to say?"

"Then don't say anything, sunshine. Fate conspired to push us together. I've never seen any valid reason for us to be apart."

Something inside her chest wrenched. That she loved him fully in return and wanted to be with him wasn't something she'd just comprehended, she'd known for quite some time. That she couldn't live here with him and leave behind the only family she had left was a hurdle they wouldn't be able to overcome. Then there was the ocean and its rolling waves. She'd miss that more than she could ever explain.

"There is just one more thing I think you'd like to see," he said gently.

She nodded, accepting his proffered hand once again to follow him through the palace, then outside through one of its many courtyards. It wasn't until they stepped through a pathway that led to the desert farther out that she froze and stared.

"What do you think?" he asked, amusement an undercurrent in his voice.

"You built a pool out here?" she squeaked. And not just any pool. It had to be easily the length of two Olympic sized pools and twice as wide.

He nodded. "I did. And I had the mature date palms helicoptered into position around the pool to help keep the water cool."

"It's like an oasis," she said, eyeing the clumps of date palms he'd had planted around the edges to form large patches of shade on the water. A smile played at her lips. "You've even added a beach and more trees for shade."

He nodded. "I wanted to emulate the ocean as much as possible, which is why it has a salt water cell."

"It's impressive," she conceded. But it still wasn't quite the ocean she loved.

He wrapped an arm around her waist and drew her close. "And yet you sound less than impressed?"

He lifted his other arm to someone in the distance. The next second, a decent-sized wave formed and traveled across the pool before splashing against the beach and retreating back into the water.

"You built a wave pool?" she asked in a voice that barely made it past a squeak. She looked up at him. "Why would you do that?"

"I did it for you," he said with a wide smile. "And for any students you might want to coach, *if* you want to continue doing so. Otherwise this wave pool is all yours."

"You've made the impossible, possible," she said in a shaky, disbelieving voice. "I can't believe you've gone to such extraordinary lengths," she added, tears now distorting her vision.

His arm squeezed her tight. "I'd do a whole lot more to keep you here with me," he said.

Her breath quickened. "I have family—

"I've offered your brother a position here if he wants it—once he's fully recovered. His family would of course share a suite of rooms with him."

"You'd do that for him?"

"I'm doing it for *you*."

"You really must love me," she said in a shaky voice.

He drew her around to face him. "I was meant to do this in the ballroom," he said, dropping onto one knee. "But what better place than right here to propose to you?"

She stared down at him, her knees going weak and her mouth dry.

He looked up at her. "I love you more than I can put into words, but hopefully my actions prove just how much I really *do* love you." He pulled a small box out of his pocket and unsnapped its lid, revealing a beautiful diamond ring. "Amber Clayton, will you marry me?"

Tears were running down her face when she threw herself into his arms, knocking the ring and its box onto the sand as she sprawled over him. "Yes!" She shouted, then sniffled and laughed before staring into his eyes and adding, "I love you too. I've loved you for the longest time."

His eyes glowed as he reached up and thumbed away her tears. "I know," he said softly, reverently. "And it nearly killed me knowing that my love was reciprocated and yet we were no longer together."

She bent and kissed him, his mouth under hers feeling so incredibly right and familiar. She pulled back with joy filling her to overflowing. "We have a lot of making up to do."

He nodded and pushed to his feet, then scooped her up into his arms. "Starting now," he said, before he strode with her back inside the palace and into his—*their*—suite of rooms.

Epilogue

Three months later...

Amber stood at the shallow end of the pool as Zach caught the small wave that began to roll through at the deep end. Kneeling on his surfboard, Katie stood balanced in front of him in her life vest, her squeal of laughter matched only by Zach's joy.

Her niece had never been happier, and lived for her moments in the surf pool with either her dad or Amber. It was all too apparent Katie took after her aunt with her love for water and surfing, while Rachel was more than happy to indulge in a day spa or roaming the palace admiring its many rooms.

Everything had fallen into place. Zach had faced the traumas of his past, which had triggered his gambling addiction, and with some therapy and a lot of soul searching his compulsion had been stifled, his focus now on his family and his new career as Basam's head accountant.

Amber shuddered. She couldn't imagine being stuck in an office all day juggling numbers, but it was Zach's passion and he was brilliant at it. Even better was that his now six-year-old daughter Katie was loving school at the palace with the couple of dozen other children who lived there with their parents.

Zach headed toward Amber and she reached for Katie and plucked her from the board, then wheeled her around in the air to more gales of laughter. "You're a natural!" she praised.

"I'm gunna be just like you when I'm older!" Katie said gleefully.

Zach tucked the board by his side and Amber walked with him through the shallows, with Katie in her arms. Zach glanced at her. "You're a great sister and an even greater auntie, but I think you're going to be an amazing mother one day."

She nodded. It'd only been a few weeks since she'd married the love of her life, then danced in his arms inside the ballroom he'd created especially for her. The reception food, created by his famous chef,

Samuel Conray, had been magical, as had the live musicians with the belly dancers.

But although she wanted almost desperately to have Basam's babies, she wanted to first experience travel and as much one-on-one time with her husband as possible with him leading his busy life as a sheikh.

"One day," she agreed with a smile.

He slowed a little as they stepped onto sand. "Please tell me you don't secretly worry you'll turn out like our parents? You're the most loyal and responsible person I know."

She play-slapped his shoulder. "That might be the nicest thing you've said to me."

Zach paused and turned to her. "I don't know where I'd be right now if it wasn't for you."

"You can thank Basam for that, not me."

"Did I hear my name?"

She turned and watched her husband stroll toward them in casual loose pants and a white top, his energy and obvious love for her making her melt. "You always seem to appear when people are singing your praises," she teased.

"Is that what you were doing?" he asked, one dark eyebrow cocked.

Before she could answer he bent and pretend-tickled Katie. "How's my little monster going?"

Katie laughed uncontrollably, then sobered quickly and asked, "We're still going for a camel ride tomorrow, Uncle Basam?"

"Of course we are! Just you try and stop me!"

Amber placed Katie on her feet as Zach grabbed the two towels left on a deck chair, then wrapped his daughter in one. Her brother's eyes shone. "You two are spoiling her rotten."

"You're only young once," Amber said softly.

Her brother nodded, then took his daughter's hand and set off into the palace to find his wife. It was lovely that Rachel was no longer the emotional wreck she'd been just a few short months ago. She was blossoming in this no stress environment and loving life once again.

"Is it too soon to sweep you off your feet and ravish you on our bed?"

"You mean to say we need a bed now?" she asked. They had, after all, utilized just about every piece of furniture in their suite of rooms. "Perhaps I could hang from the chandelier while you—"

"Stop," he growled. "Soon I'll be so hard I'll be tenting my pants."

She giggled. "I only have to flutter my lashes and you're erect."

He drew her in for a kiss, his lips soft and pliant, but his intentions clear. "And you wouldn't have it any other way."

He was right, she wouldn't. He was perfect.

Life was perfect.

Want even more sheikh stories by Mel Teshco?
Look out for Sons of the Sheikh! A brand new series coming soon in 2024!

Scorpion

His sting is as lethal as his charm

Sheikh Aziz Hadi might be a player who knows how to charm the panties off women, but that means very little when the one woman he wants—Zamira Fasih—is also the one woman he can't have. She's the daughter of a sheikh from a neighboring country bordering his province. That they're at war means there is no way he can talk to her, let alone date her. Then he sees her at the markets and he can't deny the impulse to take what—*who*—he wants.

Zamira Fasih is not interested in Aziz, at least that's what she tells herself. He and his family sided with an enemy of her father's and now her people are paying the ultimate price. The Hadi family are scum, and Aziz is the worst of them. He's not worthy of her attention, if only she'd stop damn well thinking about him! Then he kidnaps her and expects her to like him—he'd better think again!

She is promised to another man who will help end the war and the death of her people, and nothing will change her mind. Not even the famous scorpion charm Aziz is renowned for.

In the meantime...check out my new mafia series, Wedlocked.

Chapter One of Wedlocked

The euphoria slipping over me like a second skin was nothing short of liberating as I sashayed my way through throngs of glittering guests, surreptitiously eavesdropping on their conversations while I sipped on overpriced bubbles.

I was born for this subterfuge...for the thrill of the hunt. Except, I was no hunter, I wasn't even a spy. Hell, I wasn't even meant to be here tonight.

I was Sabrina Costa, the one and only daughter of the Costa mafia family. Not only was I invaluable, a pawn to my family, I'd become somewhat invisible, too. I could put up with being a pawn—weren't we all?—but it grated my gears that I'd never been allowed to bask in the power and prestige given freely to my brother, Salvatore.

I was determined that would change tonight and I'd be the one who'd uncover what was really going down with our rival mobster family, the Agostinos.

A shiver of unease threatened to take away my swagger. If my father or my brother caught me here at our rival's house, I'd never be without a guard again. Hell, there was a chance I mightn't even make it out of this party alive, if my own family didn't kill me first.

The knowledge sent my pulse racing, my breath catching in the throat. A smile curled my lips. Damn, it was good to finally feel alive! Being groomed to be the next bride to some Frankenstein mobster wasn't my one and only objective in life. *That* was pretty much last on my bucket list.

I was determined to prove one way or another that I wasn't just a pretty face. I had power too, along with connections, they were just more...subtle. I touched my plump, lower lip. One didn't need to fire a semi-automatic when poisoned lipstick could do the job with so much more...finesse.

Not that I was planning on killing anyone tonight. Information was all I desired. After all, information was power and I craved that rush like nothing else, craved to experience what my brother did on a daily basis.

Being a woman hadn't curbed my killer instincts, if anything it'd honed them sharper. I wasn't a behind-the-scenes type of woman, I never had been. I might have been homeschooled and kept socially inept, but it hadn't dulled my brain. My teachers had quickly learned I was bright. Too bright at times for the social role I'd one day soon be forced to play—an arranged marriage to propel my mafia family's standing to the top of the heap once and for all.

I had a fair idea now which man out of the three other mobster families my father planned to assign me to, and it most certainly wouldn't be one of the Agostino brothers. My dad was already leaning toward the Accardi family underboss, anything to push back the powerful Agostino uprising.

I'd be fed to the wolves, quite literally, my virtue of no importance once my father agreed upon my worth. That I was a beauty along with being an innocent would no doubt increase my potential groom-to-be's desire to have me...to own me. And probably hurt me. It would be considered a small price to pay so that my family could wrestle back mobster dominance.

Little wonder I'd been guarded so stringently. My role as daughter had been just as important, possibly more so, than the role of my brother. It meant I'd had few friends or social interactions growing up and I'd had to strive to be adept in a crowd, playing it cool when inwardly my ego and passionate nature battled with my fragile insecurities and inexperience with social engagements.

The one benefit from my upbringing was that no one recognized me now. I was a stranger here, slipping through the party like a wraith in my wraparound, red sheaf dress and silver heels. I'd ensured my striking platinum blonde hair, a trait I shared with Salvatore, was pulled off my face in a braided topknot. I hadn't had time to do much of anything else. Even my lipstick had been applied hastily in the back of the cab I'd ordered to pick me up a block away from my family home.

The Agostinos lived an hour west of New York City, their house overlooking the same Promenade River that my family's house did. Except us Costas lived an hour east of New York. It didn't stop the turf rivalry between us. It was legendary and spanned generations thanks to our forebears who'd moved from Sicily with nothing but a gun, and whole lot of grit and determination.

"I hear Ethan won't be joining us for at least another hour."

My ears pricked at the name of the Agostino underboss, and I tuned into the gossip ensuing between the three young, designer clad women dripping with jewels and barely withheld envy.

"He's celebrating privately first, if you get my drift," said a brunette, her sparkly diamond clips holding back the sides of her dead-straight hair.

Celebrating *what*, exactly? A pity I couldn't approach and straight out ask them. Not without drawing attention to myself.

"Surely there are enough girls willing to do him for free?" a dark-haired women asked, her hands fluttering as she fanned her flushed face. "Lord knows I'd do him in a heartbeat."

"Who says he wants them willing?" the brunette asked with a husky, evocative laugh. "Besides, you'd do anyone for free," she added with a malicious sniff.

I didn't hang around to hear the rest of their mean dialogue, instead I found myself drifting around the huge marble staircase while my thoughts also drifted. I only hoped my platinum wig, which I'd left lying on top of my pillow on my bed back home, would trick anyone who might look in on me until I returned home.

It'd be unlikely anyone would bother. It wasn't like I had a mother anymore to care about me and my father most certainly didn't. As for my brother, our bond was seriously close but even he was too busy lately in his role as our father's underboss to focus on me.

No one would miss me until morning.

In the meantime I had to be careful not to engage in conversation with anyone while being mindful my distinctive hair stayed pulled back so that I didn't stand out. Another frisson of excitement sparked through me as I edged through the crowd. I was just another beautiful face amongst these wealthy and overdressed guests.

The fact I might be one of the few women here without a clutch purse or cellphone was probably more noticeable than my hair. It'd been worth it though just so that I had no identification on me, no proof to get me caught out.

This is stupid! Reckless. Dangerous.

"And I wouldn't change a thing," I murmured to myself as I rounded the grand staircase with its glittering chandelier hanging high above.

I stopped as I inadvertently stumbled upon a discreet service entry elevator, where a harried young waiter pushed a cart of liquor and other supplies inside, the doors then sliding shut behind him.

My belly fluttered and my womb clenched. Was that where I'd find the underboss? Ethan might not yet be the don, but it would only be a matter of time before he took over from his father.

I shuddered. Ethan's father, Lorenzo, made my own dad look like Prince Charming. Violence might be a way of life for our families, but Lorenzo was as soulless as a man could get without already being in hell.

Even I'd heard rumors about the Agostino don's proclivities. He enjoyed inflicting pain and punishment, and got off on watching others suffer. Not even his family was safe. I could only imagine the sadistic children he'd raised.

The elevator doors reopened and a suited man stepped out. His dark eyes trawling over my silver-blonde hair, he asked, "You're here for Ethan?"

I blinked, then automatically nodded as realization kicked in. The soldier presumed I'd been hired to have sex with his boss. I ran an absent hand along the silky fabric of my short, fitted gown. I hadn't intended to dress like one of Ethan's whores, but who was I to deny fate? I wanted answers, what better way to get them than straight from the horse's mouth.

The suited man's eyes glinted. "I can see now why he has a thing for blondes. That lucky bastard really is celebrating tonight."

I managed a coy smile. Fuck. Did high-priced whores act cheap or did they swan around like celebrities? The whores that my dad and brother had brought into our home hadn't exactly been subtle about their intentions. But surely discretion was what a higher-end escort provided?

I sashayed past suited-man and stepped alone into the elevator, my panties already a little damp just thinking about what could happen upstairs with Ethan if I wasn't careful. He'd be expecting pre-celebration sex, probably hardcore stuff only the most experienced of women would know how to enjoy.

I swallowed as the doors slid shut and the elevator swept me upstairs. I'd seen pictures of Ethan. He might have been good looking if not for his hard eyes and the jagged white scar spreading halfway along his jaw. If his full lower lip hinted at sexuality, the thin upper lip hinted at cruelty.

He was something of a paradox to me even before the elevator doors slid open and I was greeted with the man himself...in all his naked glory.

If you'd like to know when my next book is available, as well as other pre-orders, cover reveals and other news, sign up for my newsletter: https://madmimi.com/signups/121695/join

Check out my website – http://www.melteshco.com/

You can also friend me on Facebook at https://www.facebook.com/mel.teshco

Or my author Facebook page at https://www.facebook.com/MelTeshcoAuthor

Contact me: melteshco@yahoo.com.au

If you enjoy my books I'd be delighted if you would consider leaving a review. This will help other readers find my books ☺

About the Author

I'm an award winning author who loves to write scorching hot contemporary and science fiction romance—stories I love to read. I love working from home, where my office window looks out over our 'block' of fourteen acres with gorgeous mountain views. After enjoying a stint as a foster carer for cats, I now have seven felines to entertain me, along with two dogs and two horses. But only when I'm not distracted by my three gorgeous daughters, one of whom—a teenager *shriek*—is still living at home. As for my husband...he's still waiting for retirement.

Want more Mel Teshco books?
Contemporary
Desert Kings Alliance
The Sheikh's Runaway Bride (book 1)
The Sheikh's Captive Lover (book 2)
The Sheikh's Forbidden Wife (book 3)
The Sheikh's Secret Mistress (book 4)
The Sheikh's Defiant Princess (book 5)
The Sheikh's Fake Fiancée (book 6)
The Sheikh's Royal Widow (book 7)
The Sheikh's Temporary Girlfriend (book 8)
Desert Kings Alliance Box Set (Volumes 1-4)
Desert Kings Alliance Box Set (Volumes 5-8)
Gangsters at War
Wedlocked (book 1)
Avenged (book 2)
Enforced (book 3)
Contracted (book4)
more coming soon...
Bachelor Brothers of Sydney
Highest Bid (book 1)
Bought at Auction (book 2)
Winning Offer (book 3)
The VIP Desire Agency
Lady in Red (book 1)
High Class (book 2)
Exclusive (book 3)
Liberated (book 4)
Uninhibited (book 5)
The VIP Desire Agency Boxed Set (all 5 books in the series)
Box sets with authors Christina Phillips & Cathleen Ross
Sheikhs & Billionaires

Taken by the Sheikh
Taken by the Billionaire
Taken by the Desert Sheikh
Resisting the Firefighter
Standalone longer length titles: (50k-100k)
As I Am
Standalone novellas and short stories: (15k-40K)
Her Dark Guardian
Stripped
Clarissa
Camilla
Selena's Bodyguard (also part of the Christmas Assortment Box)
Anthologies
Down and Dusty: The Complete Collection
The Christmas Assortment Box
Science Fiction
The Virgin Hunt Games
The Virgin Hunt Games volume 1
The Virgin Hunt Games volume 2
The Virgin Hunt Games volume 3
The Virgin Hunt Games volume 4
The Virgin Hunt Games volume 5
The Virgin Hunt Games volume 6
Alien Fugitives
Nero (book 1)
Jasper (book 2)
Sienna (book 3)
Damaris (book 4)
Dragons of Riddich
Kadin (prequel - book 1)
Asher (book 2)
Baron (book 3)

Dahlia (book 4)
Wyatt (book 5)
Valor (book 6)
The Queen (book 7)
Alien Hunger
Galactic Burn (book 1)
Galactic Inferno (book 2)
Galactic Flame (book 3)
Coming soon
Galactic Blaze (book 4)
Nightmix
Lusting the Enemy (book 1)
Abducting the Princess (book 2)
Seducing the Huntress (book 3)
Winged & Dangerous
Stone Cold Lover (book 1)
Ice Cold Lover (book 2)
Red Hot Lover (book 3)
Winged & Dangerous Box Set (all 3 books in the series)
Dirty Sexy Space continuity with Denise Rossetti:
Yours to Uncover (book 1)
Mine to Serve (book 6)
Ours to Share (book 8)
Awakenings series with Kylie Sheaffe
No Ordinary Gift (book 1)
Believe (book 2)
Homecoming (book 3)
Standalone longer length titles: (50k-100k)
Dimensional
Mutant Unveiled
Shadow Hunter
Existence

Standalone novellas and short stories: (15k-40K)
Identity Shift
Moon Thrall
Blood Chance
Carnal Moon